To Gloria,
I hope you
like book two!
-Jacob Buckley

The Great Mistake

The Journey Continues

By

Jacob Salpeter Buckley

Sequel to Traveling to the Fourth Dimension

authorHOUSE™

1663 LIBERTY DRIVE, SUITE 200
BLOOMINGTON, INDIANA 47403
(800) 839-8640
WWW.AUTHORHOUSE.COM

First published by AuthorHouse 10/06/04

ISBN: 1-4184-9936-6 (sc)

Printed in the United States of America
Bloomington, Indiana

This book is printed on acid-free paper.

Contents

Author's Note..viii

Part One: Mistake to the Fifth Dimension 1

1. Celebrations 3

2. The Shadow In His Room................................. 12

3. The Urgent Message 16

4. The Man in Martin's Head................................. 23

5. A Closer Look 26

6. A Secret World 29

7. Puzzle Pieces.. 35

8. The Search 44

9. A Chance to Return.. 48

10. When Darkness Calls 53

11. Another Look 60

12. The Power of Hatred.. 63

13. The Second View 68

14. Alone.. 76

15. MindLite 86

16. A Ruined Plan 92

17. The Planet with No Escape 97

18. Plans... 99

19. Questions.. 103

Part Two: Return to the Fourth Dimension 107

20. The Talk 109

21. Ruined Again 114

22. The House 118

23. The Quite Disappointing Return 121

24. The Communicator 124

25. Old Enemies...................................... 126

26. Escape? 131

27. New Hope 134

28. Fillip's Rescue Attempt............................. 136

29. Many Difficulties 140

30. Home at Last...................................... 145

Part Three: Revenge 149

31. An Old Friend 151

32. A Warm Welcome 153

33. The Beginning of Her Revenge 159

34. Fillip's Fight...................................... 165

35. The International Scientific Academy............... 167

36. Their Escape...................................... 173

37. Jace's Mistake 175

38. Getting In Mourndess' Way 177

39. The Dimensions Beyond.......................... 186

40. The Great Shattering Device.......................... 192

Part Four: A Second Chance............................ **201**

41. The Thirteenth Dimension with Jace 203

42. The Third Dimension Again 207

43. Jace's Mystery.. 213

44. Stopping the Great Shattering Device............. 217

45. The Truth.. 222

46. Their Escape from her Trap 229

47. Mourndess and the Great Shattering Device ... 233

48. A Second Chance 238

Author's Note

I am proud to say that I have finished writing my second book, The Great Mistake. It is the sequel to Traveling to The Fourth Dimension, and what I hope to be the second book in a trilogy. I felt that writing the second book was harder for me than writing the first. I had already been writing constantly for a year to finish my fist book, and I felt a need for a break. Many times I stumbled upon writer's block. Now that I am finished with book two I am glad to say that no matter how many times I told my family I was quitting for sure, I managed to pull through to the end.

I had no lack of support when writing this book, particularly from my family, friends, classmates, and teachers. First, I would like to thank my mother, Shelley Salpeter, for taking the time to edit the book, and for being my manager and publicist. I also want to thank my brother, Nick Buckley for reading my book many times to proofread it, and also for helping me write, even when my mind was set on doing something else. I would also like to thank Carol Wilson for tirelessly editing the book and Jack Kastrop for proofreading it.

And many thanks to my father, Doug Buckley and my grandfather, Ed Salpeter, who read through the book and gave helpful comments.

I would then like to thank my nanny Laura Cardenas, for encouraging me to write consistently, no matter how many times I forgot to. There are many others who have helped or supported me, and for those who I have not mentioned, thank you. I have good feelings about starting my next book, The Right Choice, and I hope to finish that over the next year. My goal in life is not to be particularly famous or even well known as an author; it's to be proud of each book I manage to write. I also hope that whoever chooses to read my book will enjoy it.

☺I hope you like the book!☺

This book is dedicated to my grandmother, Mika Salpeter and my old dog, Maxwell Smart. Both of you were in my heart as I wrote this book, and I felt your friendship and warmth. I want to thank you both, for the many lessons in life I have learned from you. I still love both of you dearly and want you to know that wherever you are, this book is for you.

October 6, 3459, 8:49 A.M.

Celebrations

1

The creature crept through the grass when its prey was facing away, and flew in the air when the prey's back was turned. Slowly the creature moved closer and closer to its target. As it moved, it thought of how this was proof to all that size doesn't matter when it comes down to hunter and victim. It watched as its victim was talking to his family, unaware of the horrors that awaited him. Closer and closer the creature crept, until it was time to swiftly rise into the air, then strike.

"Tag you're it!" Jess yelled playfully into Fillip's ear. Fillip spun around looking utterly aghast.

"That's not fair!" Fillip said, with both hands clenched in tight fists on his hips.

"You're only saying that because you're unhappy that I found you in your lame hiding spot," Jess said, testing Fillip's nerve.

"No! Anyone that knows anything could see that I was talking to my dad!"

"Hiding."

"Talking."

"Hiding."

"No, talking!" Fillip was so caught up in the argument that he didn't notice the message Jess was giving Dan with her movements.

"Hiding."

"Talking."

"Hiding."

"Taallkkkiinnnngggggggggg!!!!!!!!!!!!!!!!!!!!!"

"Fine then, if this means so much to you, let's just start again with Dan being it."

"Fine." With that Fillip turned around to see Dan waiting right behind him with his arm out, just barely touching Fillip's left shoulder.

"Tag," Dan said with a smile.

Later that day, Fillip was still grumpy about the game of tag. He could be found somewhere in his room, muttering things about unfair play, just talking to Dad about something, absolutely no secret messages to other players, and no cheating or teaming up on other players. After about an hour of not being able to study because of the annoying grumbling coming from the room next to him, Dan got up out of his seat and went over to his brother's room. When Dan entered the room, Fillip looked up at his brother with a sour, unfriendly look.

"What do you want?" he asked sullenly.

"Okay, if this is so important to you, tell me; what were you talking to Dad about?"

"Well, I had been thinking that our family is happy enough right now, and that Mathonog and Soseph don't seem to be doing a very good job of chasing after us anyway." The previous year their father, Martin Westle Parnes, had met his future self through a time warp and learned that there was a fourth dimension, which overlaps with the third dimension every few million years. He also discovered that dimension warps could appear while they were overlapping. After Martin had found a warp, he had connected the third and fourth dimensions and the entire world's population had gone through the warp.

Unfortunately, Martin and his sons Dan and Fillip did not receive a warm welcome from the inhabitants, especially two men named Mathonog and Soseph. In fact, these men were almost as concerned about catching and killing Martin as they were in finding the mysterious Shattering Device. The Shattering Device was a color-changing shape-shifting ship that seemed to have a mind of its own and had many devices within it, one of which was very important to Mathonog and Soseph. Martin still pondered at night about what horrors would await them if Mathonog and Soseph ever got what they wanted. So far they had failed to get both the Shattering Device and Martin, but that was not a reason to stop worrying completely.

Mathonog and Soseph were actually born in the sixth dimension, and they were very much like humans. The exceptions were that their eyes were of a very pale color and they had higher IQs than most humans, at least in terms of their ability to invent new things. Last year, a few of the people who worked with Martin at Future Discoveries had decided to stay behind in the fourth dimension to perform research, despite the risks and uncertainties. Martin was constantly thinking about them and was always afraid that Mathonog and Soseph would somehow harm them.

Whenever anyone stepped through a warp in the fourth dimension, a new copy of that person was created. To help counter this effect Martin had given his friends a Unifier, which deletes the extra copies with each warp travel. Another problem with the dimension is that whenever anyone stepped through a time warp or even a dimension warp, they tended to get lost when they emerged on the other side. So, his friends carried a Retriever so they could immediately locate anyone who was lost and teleport that person back to the central area where the Retriever was kept. These two devices had been originally given to Martin by Grey when Martin had passed a test of Grey's.

Mathonog and Soseph had managed to capture Martin twice while he was in the fourth dimension, but Martin narrowly escaped both times. The first time, he was helped by his newly discovered friend, Jess, an electronic beetle who had been created by Mathonog and Soseph, but escaped before being experimented on. The second time, he was rescued by Fillip who had ingeniously used an electronic penknife that Martin had

Part One:

Mistake to the Fifth Dimension

given him for his seventh birthday. Now that he, Jess and the boys were back safely in the third dimension and things had been quiet for a while, they did not feel the threat of being attacked again by Mathonog and/or Soseph.

After a few moments of remembering the fun and excitement they had had last year, Fillip continued. "So, I thought that it would be great if we could get…a puppy."

"A puppy?" Dan repeated in disbelief.

"Yeah," Fillip answered. Dan considered this for a moment. Then he nodded and said,

"That may be a good idea, but I think we should try to find a calm puppy, maybe even a dog. Maybe it would be best if we got ourselves a two-year-old dog, at least." Fillip agreed with Dan. Since Fillip seemed to have calmed down and was deep in thought about the possibility of a new puppy, Dan went back to his room and finished his studying in peace.

When Jess heard about the puppy, she agreed immediately, as she had always wanted to have an animal friend. They told Martin about the idea, and he said that he would think about it. Martin actually felt that it was a fantastic idea for his family, and that it would be great if they could find a puppy by the next day, when they were planning to have a double birthday party for Fillip and Dan. Fillip had missed any festivities on his last birthday because Martin had been captured by Mathonog and Soseph that day. Dan had missed his because he had been lost in the fourth dimension at the time.

So, Martin took Dan and Fillip to the pound and told them to select a dog, even though he didn't tell them that they would actually be taking the dog home with them. The boys both picked a dog that looked like a puppy but acted like a grown dog. The workers at the pound said they could not tell how old it was. It was a golden retriever but there was something very odd about him. For instance, when Fillip put his hand out to pet him, the dog immediately put up a paw to shake his hand. Another time that the dog displayed his weird behavior was when Dan and Fillip asked if they could take the dog home with them. The dog started to nod pleadingly, as if he had understood every word.

When Martin said he would think about it, the dog ran over and gave him a "bambi eyes" look. It certainly seemed to be working. "We will think about it," Martin said. With a look of pure joy on his face, the dog nodded his head up and down. One of the workers looked at the dog in surprise and said that it was odd; the dog had paid no attention to all the other people he had met. They all left the pound thinking about how weird a dog it was.

The next day it was time for the festivities of their double birthday party. Fillip was belatedly celebrating his 8th birthday and Dan his 19th. Dan and his friends went to the aerial alcove and hooked up to an interactive holo-simulation, while Fillip and his friends played outside. The presents were the usual aura-books, electronic puzzles, head-speakers and the like. But the present Martin gave them was, as always, the best by far. The package was quite big and asymmetric, with a bulge on the left side. When Fillip and Dan opened it, there was a dog carrier with magnetically attached dog bowls for food and water that trains the dog to press a button for refills. But the best part of the present was currently asleep in a corner of the carrier.

"Our very own dog!" exclaimed Fillip.

"Thanks!" Dan said to Martin. They all thought that the double birthday party was a success. They sat, waiting until the dog woke. It was still small enough to hold and was very cute. Fillip simply couldn't stop hugging and petting the little dog until it fell asleep again. That night they all slept peacefully, with pleasant dreams.

The Shadow In His Room

2

The next morning when Martin woke up, he decided to begin training the dog. He walked into the living room briskly, stopping to snatch the controller as he made his way over to the carrier and he knelt down to see the dog. For some reason it did not surprise Martin to find those big blue eyes already wide open, looking at him. The dog did not howl or whine, but just sat there patiently waiting to be greeted. "Since when have puppies been patient?" Martin wondered to himself as he pressed the button to open the carrier door. Martin shook his head as he led the dog into the kitchen, got some treats, and took the dog to a lawn outside.

"Okay, let's see if this works." He took out a treat and held it behind his back so the dog could not see it.

"Stay," he commanded. He walked down the lawn and back, and then stared wide eyed at the dog. It had not moved at all, but sat still at attention.

"And all the neighbors say it takes a lot of practice," he said to no one in particular. "Good boy!" Martin said as he rewarded the dog with a treat.

"Stay." He walked to the other end of the lawn. "Come!" he said loudly enough for the dog to hear. The dog walked over to Martin obediently and sat down, waiting for a treat. Martin went through every command he could think of and the dog did every one without failure. He could fetch anything that Martin asked him to get, he could roll over, and he could stand on his hind legs on command, and even jump when he was told to.

It certainly seemed to Martin that the dog actually understood what he was saying. Martin began getting frazzled thinking of things for the dog to do; the dog just sat there shaking his head in sympathy. "What is wrong with this dog?" Martin thought. Martin tried to think of a name for the dog, but the dog did not respond to any name Martin could think of. So, the dog remained unnamed.

That night, Martin was in his bedroom still thinking about his new dog when suddenly a great pain shot through head. He felt a strong urge to destroy anything in his path, but immediately he knew what he must do. Martin forced a wall to form in his mind and all of these thoughts were blocked out. A grey swirl appeared in front of Martin. If Martin looked closely he could imagine a human form blocked out by a grey cloud, so thick that he could not see any detail at all.

"That wasn't funny, Grey," Martin said dryly.

"Oh, come on, can't I have some fun?" Grey asked.

"You will never learn...," Martin said.

"Ah, that's where you're wrong. I believe it is you who has a lot to learn about things, human!" Gray corrected with a faint hint of a smile.

"What is it this time, Grey?"

"Do you remember our last visit?" Back in the fourth dimension Martin had came across a strange ruin where he met three spirits, White, Grey, and Black. The three of them work for the High Force. They were required to work together, although they usually did not get along very well, because they were all so very different. White liked happiness and goodness, Grey loved power and, at times, destruction, and Black liked evil and badness. The ruins that Martin found in the fourth dimension are where White, Grey and Black lived, but the three entities could actually travel anywhere. After Martin passed Grey's test, Grey began to like Martin. He had visited Martin just a few days before, giving Martin a prediction that forces beyond Martin's wildest imagination would come into play soon.

"Yes I remember your last visit. What about it?"

"This is about that prediction!" As Grey slid around Martin in a flash Martin realized, not for the first time, that Grey looked just like a grey shadow. Martin rammed his body into Grey's shapeless form with all of his strength.

"What is it Grey?"

Grey shook him off and said, "I won't tell you!" Martin pictured in his mind a strong wall that would hold Grey off because he had learned how to make his mind strong, maybe even stronger than his physical self. Grey easily shattered Martin's mind-wall, and proceeded to give him a massive headache. Martin dropped to the floor, his concentration lost. Just as Grey was about to slide out of the room, Grey turned a bright shade of gold and stayed like that for a second, frozen in place. And then he disappeared.

The Urgent Message

3

Martin was in the living room, drinking colart, a drink that can clear a headache in a few seconds and comes in the flavor of any drink imaginable. Martin was at that moment drinking a strawberry fizzle colart and rubbing his head. He started to think about that day last year at the dimension warp, when everyone from Earth had already gone back to the third dimension. Actually, it had been everyone except for Martin, Fillip, Dan, Jess, Arnold Frizt, Lemmy Harp, Jones Walter, Jenna Gruvitz, and Marie Danica. All five of his friends from Future Discoveries had decided to stay in the fourth dimension. Before Martin had returned to the third dimension his friends had given him a communicator that would allow them to talk with each other through the two dimensions, and Martin kept it in his pocket at all times.

Martin also started to think about that day, long before he had ever dreamed of dimension travel, when he and his friends first found the Connector. They had picked it up, brought it back to Future Discoveries and called it the new prototype, until Martin learned from his future self that it was actually a device that could connect the different dimensions. It was an ancient-appearing wooden device that was shaped like an old-fashioned time-piece but instead of hands it had two spheres, one labeled 3rd and one labeled 4th.

When Martin had finally returned to the third dimension after his journey to the fourth dimension, he was so afraid that someone was going to steal the device that he had created an elaborate security mechanism for the machine. This mechanism consisted of a three-button combination code that allowed a password to be entered. If the correct password was entered, a complex set of sockets appeared that allowed for wires to be connected in a certain order. Only then would the warp appear. He kept the wires hidden in one set of titanium drawers and the Connector in another drawer, all locked with two sets of keys. Martin kept those keys with him at all times. So far he had not needed the security, but you could never be sure these days.

Still rubbing his head, Martin got up. The headache had completely disappeared but he still felt a strange ringing in his ears, so he decided to take a walk. He went into Dan's room and saw both Fillip and Dan together. Fillip was lying on his bed, playing with the puppy. Dan was reading an aura-book on astronomical travel. That reminded him.

"When are you planning on getting a job?" Martin asked Dan. Dan looked up from his book.

"I will get a job as soon as I'm done with my studies," Dan replied calmly. After Martin's discovery of the fourth dimension, all schools had stopped teaching. Now that everyone had returned, the schools were starting up again.

"What would you like to be, Dan?" Martin asked.

"I'm thinking about being an astrophysicist. I have decided I am going to study at the Stockholm Astronomical Institute, starting at the beginning of the year." Dan had always been a good student, and had finished his undergraduate studies with honors. He had already applied to several different graduate programs in different subjects before they had left for the fourth dimension. Now that they had returned, he thought that learning about other universes and dimensions would be fun.

"Stockholm? That's marvelous! But, isn't that a bit far away? Are you planning on living there or transporting?" Martin came over and sat down next to Dan and Fillip.

"I think the best thing would be use the transporter, and come home every night. That way I can be close to you, and keep an eye on Fillip when you are off gallivanting." Martin knew how protective Dan was of Fillip, ever since their mother had disappeared. After what they had all gone through this past year, Martin knew Dan did not feel comfortable leaving home yet, even though he was now 19 years old and starting his graduate studies.

"Why do you need to keep an eye on me?" Fillip grumbled. I'm 8 years old already. I can take care of myself!"

"You may have a point...But then again I know you can't."

"Says who?" Fillip shot back.

"To be perfectly frank with you, I do."

"I hate to break up your fun, but I'm going for a walk, okay?" said Martin, as he stood up. They both nodded. As Martin walked out of the room, he heard Fillip and Dan continue their bickering. He walked outside while shaking his head and grinning.

As he walked, he thought about Dan going off for his studies. He was never particularly happy with too many transporter usages in a short period of time after his wife, Yargentia, had been lost in a transporter accident. No one actually knew that she had died, but she hadn't been seen for four years now, and there had not been any reports of potential sightings in that time. Despite this, he almost never stopped thinking about her, and how he might get her back at any time. Martin continued on his walk, occasionally stopping to admire and smell a patch of flowers as his body took in the warm sun and the fresh air. He was awakened from his trance when he heard a low pitched loud buzz. He knew that sound only too well.

About a week ago, Arnold had called him from the fourth dimension to tell him about his discovery of what he called "normal warps". These normal warps appeared to transport someone to a random location, and had never been seen or noticed before. A wave of excitement blasted through Martin as he wondered what they had found out this time. *Martin it's me... Help...Come quickly...we're...being...taken...there is a child... come quickly...help ...*

The transmission ended suddenly, amidst loud crackling noises. Martin turned off his communicator. Mathonog and Soseph, he thought. They were going to get it this time. He ran back home quickly.

Later that day Martin left a transmission to the boys saying, "Take care of yourselves for a bit. I've got to run. I'll come back home soon." He knew it was horrible to leave his boys this way, but he had to do it. Dan and Fillip could handle it. He took out one of the silver keys and opened the titanium drawer. He took out the wire and the Connector, pressed the buttons and typed in the password. He put one end of the wire into one of sockets and was about to do the same with the other end when Dan and Fillip walked in. Martin turned to face his children, and did not realize that he had put the wire into a wrong socket.

"Dad, the super-computer is broken," Fillip complained.

"I'll be there in a minute."

"But Dad…"

"I'll be there in a minute." As they turned around, Martin looked back at the Connector and realized immediately that something was wrong, but he just couldn't tell what. He turned back to walk over to the door and at the same time Martin leaned back and pressed the button by accident. A huge warp appeared that covered the entire room, and took Martin as well as Dan, Fillip, and Jess, who happened to be perched on Fillip's shoulder. As Martin was being sucked into the warp, he realized what had been different on the Connector. Instead of having two spheres, one labeled 3rd and the other labeled 4th, there had been three. On the third one, clearly labeled and highlighted in blue, was written 5th.

The Man in Martin's Head

$\underline{4}$

Martin looked up. He was lying on a cold stone floor. He was in a room with blank purple walls. There was a red carpet lying right near him. The red carpet led his eyes up a staircase to rest upon something he did not believe possible. On the platform that the stairs led to, sitting on a throne, was a perfect replica of Martin. Was it alive? Did he actually make it into the fourth dimension? What had happened to Grey's device that eliminated extra copies of people? Those and hundreds of other questions like them formed in his head.

Martin suddenly realized that the walls weren't blank anymore. They were covered with strange posters. Martin sneaked a glance at one of the posters that read quite clearly, *Help needed. Is Martin Westle Parnes in the Fourth Dimension?* Martin blinked. The notice did not change. Martin then decided to try an experiment, and at that very moment a poster appeared reading, *Notice, Martin has decided to experiment,* which remained for a few moments and then disappeared.

Martin looked at a blank wall and thought he saw light coming in from outside. "Is it a bright day outside?" And just as he expected, a notice appeared informing him of his thoughts. Martin looked back at his copy, who was staring directly at him. *Stop playing around*, a voice in Martin's head said. Martin had no idea why that thought had come up. He didn't remember thinking it. *Oh! For heaven's sake! Look up!* Martin obeyed without question and there his eyes rested on the Martin copy. It had not moved at all.

"Where am I?" Martin asked his replica suspiciously. *Don't talk so loud! You're wasting your time with my physical form! Speak silently!*

"But how am I supp-" *Oh for heaven's sake, be quiet! Think what you have to say!*

"Where am I?" Martin thought. *Much better, you are just where I left you. Or if you prefer, you are just where you left yourself.*

"I beg your pardon?" *That does not matter right now. I have come here to-*"You didn't come here, I did! Could you please slow down and..." *SILENCE! Listen to me!*

If you want, you can always seek help.
But if you don't want to get stuck in the kelp,
Listen first, for my call,
And when you hear it, do not stall!
If your dreams do not come true,
You must hear the bell chime too!
I'll always rest in back of you.
Search carefully and you'll find a clue.
Listen to me, because a life is at stake.
If you are in danger, you must not brake.

Then right before Martin's very eyes, his replica disappeared. Martin looked around one more time. There was something lying on the ground. It was a piece of translucent paper with the words the replica had just recited to him. He folded up the piece of paper and put it in his pocket, and took one more look around. He realized that he wasn't in the same place anymore. He was outside on grass. He clearly was somewhere he had never been to before. Fillip and Dan were nowhere to be seen. Where could he be? The answer came to him like a bolt of lightning. He was in the Fifth Dimension.

A Closer Look

<u>5</u>

Martin realized that he was actually quite tired. He had a headache so he decided that trying to think right now would not be the best option. He knew he needed to find his boys and Jess. They must be around here somewhere. But he was so tired that he felt he needed to close his eyes and rest. He lay down slowly, finding the most comfortable position. Once he was comfortable enough, he closed his eyes and laid his hands down so that they did not disturb him. Slowly he drifted off into a fitful sleep.

When he looked up he was actually quite refreshed so he decided it would be time to get to work. He looked at the landscape and the colors. He was on a grassy slope. The grass had a strange teal green coloring to it and the sky was most easily described as a shade of purple. As he looked on beyond the hill he saw beautiful orange and red trees with yellow-greenish leaves. He guessed that the trees change color with the season and the leaves did not. He walked down the hill with not much trouble in spite of the steep slope. Under the sun-yellow weeds and flowers of all colors, he found a pinkish soil. It looked quite beautiful. But he still wondered where Dan and Fillip were.

Martin walked farther along into a forest. He had never felt such loneliness before. He had been very far away from people before, but never so far away into a place that he did not even believe existed! But that couldn't be true, he thought. There must be something living in this dimension. He looked all around for Dan, Fillip and Jess, but they were nowhere to be found. He returned to his hilltop.

Martin sat down with troubled thoughts. He was sure they had gone through the time warp too. Maybe he just saw the Connector show the fifth dimension because that was where he was going. Maybe you can only see the dimension that you are going to. Maybe it also showed the dimension that his boys and Jess had gone into, he just couldn't see it. And then, again, he might not be in the fifth dimension after all! But he must find Dan and Fillip. Even if they were together, they would be alone in a strange dimension! They would get killed! Or worse!

Martin knew he could trust Dan to protect Fillip, but for how long? He was also puzzled about that copy of himself and what he had said. How could there be another copy? What happened to Grey's device that he had won after taking that test? And what the heck did his copy say?

If you want, you can always seek help. But if you do not want to get stuck in the kelp, listen first, for my call, and when you hear it, don't stall! If your dreams do not come true, you must hear the bell chime too! I'll always rest in back of you, search carefully and you'll find a clue. Listen to me, because a life is at stake, if you're in danger, you must not brake.

He wondered if the copy was following him. It was best not to think of that right now. Then he heard footsteps behind him.

A Secret World

<u>6</u>

Mourndess sighed. She had just woken up from another wonderful dream about food. Her hunger seemed unbearable but she had to admit, it had gotten less painful a few months ago. She really couldn't tell how long she had been sitting there on the floor of the small capsule. As a matter of fact, she couldn't even remember moving. Her back was as stiff as a rhino's and she didn't even want to think about what condition her neck was in. She didn't know what light looked like anymore, being out in space all of this time.

In the beginning, after traveling for a day or two, she had wasted her time and energy frantically looking around inside the capsule that was just barely big enough for her. She realized that this capsule had actually been designed to hold three monkeys. But, of course, she couldn't find any food. A few days after that, she realized that she was still just as hungry as she was a few days before and wondered if she was dead. The thought seemed to have no effect, like yelling at a rock or telling someone they should meet at a secret place and then watching the one thing that marks the spot being removed. It was like trying to get a sun-tan in heavy winter gear. These thoughts would usually make Mourndess go wild with anger or concern, but this time her mind was blank.

But then she had smelled a strange tangy odor that left her wanting more. It quickly changed to a strong bitter taste and then disappeared. There was only one place that Mourndess had smelled something similar. She became infuriated at what Mathonog and Soseph had done to her. They had put a Starve M24 Chemical in her capsule. The Starve M24 is a substance that can last for a few years and creates a bubble around something, an invisible intangible bubble. She could go through the bubble and the effects of the M24 would stop. Unfortunately, though, Mathonog and Soseph had put the bubble around the capsule, so as long as Mourndess was in that capsule, she had the M24.

The Starve M24 allowed her to remain on the brink of starvation. Then, after a few years when the substance ran out or if she got out of the bubble somehow, the effects of the M24 would disappear. At that time the M24 was illegal in all dimensions, but that certainly wouldn't stop Mathonog and Soseph. Ever.

She had known the two of them since she was a young child, on that day when the world that Mourndess, Mathonog, and Soseph knew so well was destroyed, that horrible day so many years ago...But she really didn't want to think about that time right now. So instead, she thought of what the authorities would have said if they found that Mathonog and Soseph had a laboratory out in space where they grew M24. Mathanog and Soseph's laboratory had grown considerably over the years. Once it had been used as a prison for Martin Westle Parnes, that unlucky fellow who had been selected by the Shattering Device as "the one standing in the way".

The Shattering Device was the one thing that Mathonog, Soseph, and Mourndess wanted more than anything else in the world. But things had not gone as planned. Mathonog and Soseph had gotten the Shattering Device and knew, like Mourndess, the password for how to turn it on. But they did not know, as Mourndess did, that it will randomly select one creature somewhere and say that that person stood in

31

their way. Mourndess knew, of course, that this was not the truth at all; it would keep on selecting different obstacles until the end of time. She also knew that there was another password that would cause the device to skip that part completely and move on to its main use.

Sadly, Mourndess was the only one that knew of this password and what it was, and just one year ago, the Shattering Device had selected Martin. She did not care about this human in particular, but all the same, she wondered what had happened to him. She knew that he was probably dead by now, because when Mathonog and Soseph want something done, they would stop at nothing before they accomplish their task. Although she wouldn't normally admit it, they could go pretty far. Mathonog and Soseph were not people you would want to mess with. Whoever you were. Wherever you were. At any time.

Just a short while later, Mourndess saw something, something she never imagined seeing ever again. She saw land. Well, it was not the first time she had seen land because she had been out here for so long that she hallucinated a lot. But she realized, to her dismay, that even if she did crash here and was not hallucinating, no one would ever be able to get her out. The only way that she could get out was if someone said the word "endeavor" at a 20 foot distance from her capsule. The planet was probably deserted anyway. But then the moment that she had dreamed about for weeks came. Slowly she went closer and closer to the planet, until finally she could see it clearly.

McMerolin, a little kid with an amazing interest in words, was sitting on a great lawn reading a dictionary. He was into the "E"s.

"Encyst: to enclose in a cyst.

End: Either extremity of something that has length.

Endamoeba: any of several parasitic amoebas of the genus Entamoeba.

Endanger: To expose to danger or harm.

End-brain: Another word for Telencephalon, the anterior portion of the fore-brain, including the cerebral cortex and related parts.

Endear: To cause or to be held dear; make beloved or esteemed.

Endearing: Inspiring affection or warm sympathy."

At that very moment his friend, Harry, was looking up at the sky.

"McMerolin!" he cried.

"Just a second-"

"But it's important!"

"Just a second! 'Endearment: The act of Endearing.

Endeav-'"

"McMerolin! LOOK!"

"JUST A SECOND! 'Endeavor-'"

McMerolin was interrupted yet again. But this time it wasn't Harry. It was Mourndess who had just dropped from the sky and landed on him.

Puzzle Pieces

$\underline{7}$

Martin stood still with fright. He felt sure that he had heard something from behind him.

"Dad!" he heard Fillip and Dan exclaim from behind him.

"Good to see you again," he heard Jess say. Martin spun around. He hadn't been hearing things. There they were: Fillip, Dan, and Jess. Martin ran over to give each of them a hug and Jess perched herself on Martin's shoulder.

"Where have you been? I have been looking all over for you!" Martin exclaimed.

"We are not completely sure ourselves. We were each in different places to start off with, and then we met each other somewhere over there," Fillip said as he pointed a fair distance in the direction that Martin had been looking.

"Then we saw you and ran over here," Dan explained.

"I think we should now tell each other our own separate stories. That way we might have a better clue about what this place is and how we can get out," Jess suggested.

Then Martin said, "Good idea, I'll start." Martin told them what had happened to him from the start, about the strange chamber and the mysterious copy of himself and the cryptic riddle. There was a short pause as all of them thought about that part of the puzzle and then it was Dan's turn to recount his part of the story.

"I started off in a strange forested area. I tried to leave but I just couldn't move get through the trees no matter how hard I tried to push my way through. I felt like I was a mime trying to push my way through an invisible wall. Then I saw a small clearing through the trees. The invisible wall disappeared and I could make it through. I continued walking for a short while and then I too saw a copy of me. I also had problems communicating with him, and he wouldn't answer any of my questions. This is what he said:

The answer to the problem is what one knows,
Only to be heard from like the call of crows.

A being is there, if you fear,
But never worry, for help is near.
Don't be afraid to stand up to your fears,
For when you see them, they must not see your
* tears.*
Thank you again, for setting me free,
And if you are in danger, don't forget me.

"Then my copy disappeared, and I found this piece of paper that had those words on it. I pocketed it, and I looked around to see that I was at the edge of a lake just below that drop," he said, pointing to a spot where Dan, Fillip, and Jess had met up. "Then after getting a quick drink, I walked just a bit before meeting up with Jess and Fillip." There was another pause as everyone thought about what they had been told again.

"That isn't even a sentence! *Only to be heard from like the call of crows.* That makes no sense whatsoever!" Fillip exclaimed.

"I know, but that's what was written on this piece of paper." Dan said.

Then Fillip told them his part. "Well, after the warp came that filled the room, I saw that the word "5th" that was flashing on the Connector. I guess that means that we're in the fifth dimension, doesn't it? So anyway, after that I found myself lying on cement. I looked around, and then realized that I was in some kind of a ruin. There seemed to have been some kind of a tower there in the past, but it was hard to tell because it was mostly crumbled and lying on the ground. That was the only thing I saw.

"Then as I started to look for you, I began to run and I slammed into some type of an invisible wall, just my luck! Then I saw a hallway with a copy of me sitting on a throne-chair down at the end. That was not fair! The only person that should be me is me, here in this place they seem to think that the only me is him! I mean, what is he doing sitting on MY throne-chair anyway? That should be me sitting there. If he wants to be me, then he can be MY peasant, not the other way round! I wanted to sit in the throne-chair!

"So anyway, before I got the chance to go over and show this guy a thing or two, this guy who was clearly me, he told me to speak from my mind. Well, at first I had no idea what he, or I, was talking about. But then I understood he meant for me to just think and he would understand me. Then he, or I, went off into another one of those riddles:

> *The enemy you see is the friend you know.*
> *I am your weapon just as stopping makes you*
> *   go.*
> *A blind man is the one who sees,*
> *Just hear don't look and you will feel my tears.*
> *Don't worry 'bout me, good buddy you're free,*
> *I might soon get caught, but*
> *By then you will know who is to be sought.*
> *Time is the key, you will soon be free.*

"Then my copy disappeared, which was pretty cool, but he left this piece of paper with those words written on it! That wasn't cool! Why did he get to make up that riddle instead of me, that I didn't even understand? I put it in my pocket anyway. Then, I found myself near a pool of water inside a forest near where Dan had found himself. I came out and that is where the three of us met up," Fillip finished. Here was another pause.

Then Jess spoke up, "I had a part too. It went like this. After the flash I saw myself at a gigantic fountain. I went over to perch on some dry rock near the base, and I came face to face with a copy of myself, just like you all did. Now I know that most beetles all seem alike to you humans but not for us beetles. This beetle was definitely a copy of me. Then it immediately started talking right inside my head, telling me to talk with my mind. After quite a lot of tries I got it. Then, just like with you, it broke off into a riddle:

> *With bits of the middle, you'll not get far;*
> *I give you a beginning, so that you'll be the star.*
> *Please beware, great fires will come,*
> *Think with wisdom, or you will be numb.*
> *Find the meaning of your dream,*
> *However scary it may seem.*
> *Think clearly and touch if you dare,*
> *When the moon meets the shadows and daylight is rare.*
> *The next puzzle clue will fly to you.*

"Then the copy disappeared and I stored the riddle in my memory banks. Than I came to this creek somewhere in between where Dan found himself and where Fillip found himself. I went out into that clearing a bit to the right and found Fillip, so I flew over there and followed him to Dan and then Martin."

There was another silence. Than Fillip pounded the ground with his fist,

"I HATE THIS! I WANT TO GO HOME! WE ALL WANT TO GO HOME! BUT HERE WE ARE, SITTING HERE READING THESE SILLY LITTLE RIDDLES THAT BARELY EVEN RHYME AND MAKE NO SENSE AT ALL. THIS IS DEFINITELY NOT THE SOURCE OF OUR ESCAPE!

"WHY ARE WE STUCK HERE ALONE IN THE 5TH...WHO ACTUALLY KNOWS WHERE WE ARE? WE DON'T EVEN KNOW HOW WE GOT HERE! WHERE IS THAT WARP, ANYWAY? WHAT ARE WE DOING LISTENING TO THIS NONSENSE? WE SHOULD HAVE FOUND THE WARP BY NOW!"

Fillip stormed about, scowling and clenching his fists. Finally he tired out, breathed heavily, sat

41

down and looked at Martin with what he hoped was a glass-shattering stare. Martin luckily did not shatter. Instead, he did what he was very good at, a thing he had a lot of experience with, something he did a lot: he set his youngest son straight.

"I know that this is...hard." He winced; hard was probably a bit of an understatement according to the mood that Fillip just showed, but he had already started so he was not about to stop now. Then he continued,

"None of us have any very positive thoughts about the situation that we are in. I bet that all of us could say much worse about it than you just did. I am not saying that you have to be calm under these conditions. But I think that if you truly mean what you just said, that you should try to contain your feelings. I know this is a little harsh, and I know that right now you could do with almost anything but a scolding so I'll tell you now that a scolding is not what you are about to receive. It is just that right now our only chance of survival could depend on whether or not we have our heads on straight.

"I know you don't think that these riddles could be of value to us, but you have to realize that they are the only things we have right now. We are farther away from home than humans thought possible a few years ago. We have no food, proper shelter, and probably no good water. We have no idea what type of creatures live in this place or their capabilities. But when it all comes down to the question of what I would put my trust in, it would be these riddles. I know that might sound crazy but it is only chance of getting out of here because, it is all we have got."

The Search

_8_

Soseph sprang up, filled with energy. Today was the day that his scan for Martin would be completed. Once, after a very faithful electronic octopus of his had nearly blown Martin up about a year ago, Martin had gone back in time and ruined Soseph's plans. What Martin did not know, however, is that Soseph's little creature had gotten a scan of Martin before Soseph had to make his escape. This scan could find the exact location of anything that it was searching for, and then could track it for several hours, giving Soseph time to go and find it.

Soseph walked over to a room that looked like a kitchen created for a mad scientist, which in Soseph's case, was not too far from the truth. There was a table that was long enough to hold about twenty people, and was covered with a strange platinum-rubber substance. There was a rusty red-colored freeze-tank, which was shaped somewhat like an amoeba.

Instead of windows, there were crooked holo-images of a flower garden that were repeated along the walls. At each end of the room there was a sturdy blue stand that held a small red ball of what felt like a softened piece of chalk. It felt soft and brittle but when squeezed, felt as hard as any metal. It was attached to headphones and visor, and had a wire with a button attached. Soseph could put this contraption on and when he pushed the button he could hear and see anything that what went on in his massive space station that he called his home. His home station was presently set afloat in the space of the fourth dimension.

But there was another use for this little red ball that only Mathonog and Soseph knew about. There was a hidden button in the table, that if pressed while simultaneously squeezing the red ball, a hallway opened up to reveal Soseph's secret laboratory. Mathonog had his similar house-in-a-capsule elsewhere. Mathonog was already seated at the table, ready for business.

"Good morning," Soseph said to him cheerily. "Are you ready to start?" Mathonog nodded. They opened up the secret portal and walked along a dim, grey hallway. They entered a massive room filled with gadgets and machinery of all kinds. They sat down at one of the few desks that were not occupied by papers and devices. The laboratory was illuminated by a glowing red ceiling.

"I'll go get the scanner," Mathonog said, and with that, he hurried off. When he got back, he held the electronic octopus with a monitoring device attached. Soseph pushed a button and a screen appeared. When a timer counted down to zero, the screen lit up with a full set of coordinates. Within seconds they had traced the coordinates, but they made no sense at all. It said that Martin was in the fifth dimension! After they had verified the coordinates once more, Soseph spoke up, "I'll go down there and get rid of him once and for all!"

"No," Mathonog replied.

"Why not?"

"Because you have been after him for a year and it's time he got a taste of me. I know the fifth dimension better than anybody. I will get him this time, and get him for good." What Mathonog said had made sense. After a pause, Soseph agreed that Mathonog would go to the fifth dimension to destroy Martin.

Mathonog went back to his place to prepare himself for a trip to the fifth dimension to seek and destroy Martin. Martin was soon to be in some very serious trouble. Martin was feeling quite optimistic at this very moment about getting back home. If only he knew how wrong he was.

A Chance to Return

9

Mourndess lay still for a second, not really knowing what to do. McMerolin was lying sprawled on the ground, dazed and confused. He had been reciting the dictionary, and a woman had dropped from the sky and landed on top of him. He had always thought that reading a dictionary was one of the safest things he could do.

"How did..." Mourndess started. Then she looked at the book. "Yes! That's it! You were reading the dictionary, the E's! Thank heaven for the silly people like you who would waste their time doing something as useless as that!" She actually gave the boy a hug.

"Hey, it's not pointless, it...it...it's fun. I'm not silly!" but Mourndess completely ignored him.

"Now I need to find out where I am," Mourndess said.

"You know, I could help you with that," McMerolin pointed out. At that point Mourndess was already gone.

The next few minutes Mourndess spent walking through some of the most beautiful, amazing landscape she had ever seen in her life. Not that she cared at all; that kind of thing never really interested her. But she did find herself happy to be there. Eventually she found a town. In the town she saw humans…and giants and squid-like creatures and elfish creatures. She saw more different species than you could see people on rush-hour in New York City in 3459! Multiple eyes, mouths, ears, noses, and facial parts she had never even imagined were found on some creatures. Some creatures looked more like screws with springs and circular wings that could hover in the air. She found a few of them to be ingenious creations.

When Mourndess was a young girl living in the sixth dimension, she imagined what it would be like with so many different creatures trying to live together. She also imagined that there would be a lot of fighting going on, fighting and battles and destruction. But what Mourndess saw that stood out even more than the gigantic beautiful landscape, or the creatures, or the fact that she was here in the first place, was what she felt. Peace. Absolute peace. There was more peace and happiness than Mourndess had ever seen or dreamed of in her whole life.

At first it was a little awkward. Mourndess was far more comfortable with the idea of chasing after enemies, and even would be agreeable with the suggestion of a bit of torture. But after a few minutes in the town, she started to feel happier and even smile. The town was clean and beautiful, without cars or pollution, litter or smoke. Everyone walked, slithered or flew to where they were going or were transported by someone who was bigger than them.

The more she learned about the place, the more amazed she was. Everyone was always willing to help and no one was greedy. People and creatures would exchange hugs or greetings, as well as food and shelter. There were no shops, and no money. Everything was shared. By this point the Starve M24 from Mourndess' capsule had begun to wear off, and she was famished. She ate and ate, like she had never eaten before.

Wherever she went, she was offered food and drink of all kinds. And, the food was truly marvelous.

The planet, or whatever this was, was very organized and yet no one was a leader or had a higher rank than anyone else. If anyone had a suggestion or thought, they would speak their mind and everyone would talk about it until there was agreement. No one had any more say than another did. Another strange thing about the place was that everyone understood each other even though they spoke different languages. Each individual would be able to hear and understand in their own language.

It was both wonderful and eerie. Mourndess still felt a bit disappointed that there wasn't anyone she could fight or anything she could destroy. She had been sent in a pod through space where she was in a perpetual state of starvation and now she was in a world which looked a bit like paradise. She couldn't believe herself, so immediately she tried to feel more grateful and started looking around.

It didn't take much walking before she heard a voice directed to her, "I haven't seen you around, are you new here?" Mourndess spun on her heels. It was a human woman about 40 years old. She was about Mourndess' height and her face was filled with laughter lines. She seemed to be happy and in shape and her eyes spoke kindness. This woman certainly looked nice enough, and Mourndess thought that maybe the woman could help her learn more about this place and how to get home. Mourndess knew that this would be too bland a life for her. She enjoyed much more excitement in her life, but most of all she needed to get back because she had a lesson to teach Mathonog and Soseph.

"If you like, I'll show you around. My name is Yargentia."

When Darkness Calls

10

"The fifth dimension!" Mathonog muttered. That earthling had surprised him yet. After Mathonog had gotten over his excitement about finding Martin on the scan, he thought about the significance of Martin making it to the fifth dimension. If they can make it to the fifth dimension, then theoretically they could make it to any other dimension in existence! "This is bad," he thought. "Who knows what those humans will do to the dimensions when they feel like a little exploration."

Mathonog considered himself significantly more cultivated and advanced evolutionally from humans, and generally superior in all ways. In truth, Xalpons were different from the humans mainly in their capability for invention, and slightly quicker reflexes. In physical appearance they were usually about half a foot taller than a human and their fingers and toes were slightly longer. They also had a bit more control over their physical appearance, such as changing their height or eye color, and had more immunity to cancer viruses.

At that moment the holo-message display button on Mathonog's computer started flashing and made that loud beeping noise. It was Soseph.

"I got a fresh scent of the Shattering Device. I'm on your radar; just follow behind until you catch up, okay?" And with that, the screen flashed off. With Soseph, the conversations were generally one-sided like that. Mathonog didn't mind. He got in his pod, flipped on the radar and took off. To his dismay, Soseph was about 500,000 miles off. He was moving at about 750,000 miles per hour. Both Mathonog and Soseph had become expert drivers with these pods when they were still children. They had been improving their models and skills since.

To show off his new pod, Mathonog cranked it up to about 1,300,000 miles per hour and waited for the blast of colors. The pod was just about flawless. It could avoid hitting anything and would even shove that thing to one side if things got too dire. It probably couldn't move a planet but it would have no problem with a comet or asteroid, no matter what the speed.

The speed you were going at did not matter because the stability was perfect and would curve perfectly. It was not without danger but their skill was greater than any danger posed.

Mathonog finally reached Soseph, and shortly they caught up with the Shattering Device. There were no human words to accurately describe the Shattering Device. The closest you could get was an amazing, giant shuttle in many colors. In short, it was a sight that was truly unforgettable. It was incredible.

Mathonog, Soseph and Mourndess had been after the Shattering Device for thirty years. Just before everything in their world was destroyed and they started their new life in the fourth dimension, their forefathers gave them their quest: to seek out and use the device. They were happy in the fourth dimension with all the comforts they would need, but they didn't get too attached to it for they knew that all that could change. All they had to do was get the Shattering Device and successfully put it to their use, and then they could return to their realm. The dimensions would probably be destroyed in the process, but that would be acceptable if they achieved their goal.

That is what they believed the Shattering Device was originally made for, but they really weren't sure because the creators were destroyed a long time ago. Since that time the Shattering Device had begun to evolve, and was clearly being evasive. Only Mathonog, Soseph, and Mourndess could use the device because they were the only ones who knew the code. They were the only remaining Xalpons and had studied their ancestors enough to know that, at least. They believed that whoever actually used the machine would be rewarded with great power. For that reason Mathonog and Soseph had been competing fiercely with Mourndess for so many years.

They now had the device in their grasp, and they would try anything to get the machine under their control. In unison both Mathonog and Soseph shot off everything they had to hold the ship down. They had actually succeeded in catching the ship one time before, but then it got away. They tried to wrap the ship in invisible-bonds-metal-chains that seemed to wrap around it forever without significantly slowing it down. They tried to slow its movement with force fields, and also tried to leach out as much energy as they could from the engines, but the Shattering Device did not slow down.

Finally, when they were able to make strong contact, they towed it back in as fast as was safe. About two hours later, they reached Mathonog's laboratory and kept the ship in a very secured place. They left it to sit there until its engines cooled down enough so that it was safe to be near. That would take a day or two.

Two days later, they got to work on the Shattering Device. They once more tried what they had tried not that long ago. Again they got the same answer. The machine would not let them do what they wanted, because it said that Martin Westle Parnes stood in its way. They believed that Martin was probably still in the fifth dimension. Mathonog had been preparing to go there and kill Martin, but then Soseph had called with news of the Shattering Device.

Mathonog and Soseph knew they did not have much time with the machine. It clearly had a mind of its own and did not like to wait around in one place much. Over and over again Mathonog and Soseph tried to direct it but their efforts were fruitless. They kept on trying. The machine kept on responding that Martin was still alive and that he was standing in the way of them using the device. Then they heard a cold drawl from behind them,

"The Shattering Device won't work because Martin IS still around. You both know that he is in the fifth dimension." Both of them turned around and were faced by Black, with that cool black haze around him. "If you want it to listen to you, you will have to find Martin and kill him. I want just what you do, although all of us know that you are the only ones who can actually do it. You two are the only ones that know the code, except for Mourndess, of course."

That brought a chuckle from Soseph, "That will not really have to be taken into consideration, because Mourndess won't be doing much of anything for a while now." Black said nothing.

Then Mathonog said, "Wait, but don't you know the code?" Black seemed to stare right through him, even though he couldn't see eyes beyond the black haze.

Black said, "Yes, but I am not allowed to interfere with these things." Then he spoke again. "You must understand that it will never do what you tell it to you if you try to master it. It has a mind of its own and can always say no. Let it be your Master and do what it says. Then it is up to it what happens next. I'm sorry, but in truth not even I know everything about the Shattering Device; it has changed too much from its original self. Originally it was quite simple and had nothing more than one button and a control panel, with room to expand. Now, it has hundreds of buttons, is very difficult to catch, and is even picky about its users. But this much I do know, its main control still works the same, the old code hasn't changed. That's all I can tell you." And then, Black disappeared.

"I'll go now," said Mathonog. "We must destroy Martin as soon as possible and then find the machine again". They both knew that as soon as they left the Shattering Device would disappear, even if they had it tethered in place.

Another Look

11

Martin and Jess stopped and waited for Dan and Fillip to catch up. It was getting late. The sun had already fallen behind the horizon. They had just finished descending a steep slope and there were a few trees where they could sleep. They were all exhausted and hungry. They had seen plenty of unusual objects that could pass as edible, but they decided that they wouldn't try any of them

When Fillip and Dan caught up, they all lay down and tried to get some sleep despite their rumbling stomachs. They each took some alimental tablets that Martin had with him, which could tide them over until they could eat. Finally their minds slipped away to sleep. Martin found that he was sitting in the stone room again and to his dismay, he also saw his copy on that throne of his.

"What do you want?" Martin said coldly. *Well how am I supposed to know when you won't even listen to yourself on the outside, let alone your inside?*

Now I've got to say, I'm being considerably patient with you, but don't expect it all the time, only here.

"I deleted all the extra copies of me in the Fourth Dimension! How do you still exist?" Martin demanded of the copy. *I'm no copy! I'm the original! I've been working with you side by side before you knew how to think. Come on, tell me you remember me!*

"I know nothing of you; I've never worked with you either!" Martin said, starting to get a little defensive. *I guess knowledge of my existence does usually wear away with age.* Martin's copy was starting to get annoying.

"Just forget about it! Tell me what I'm supposed to do!" Martin cried out. *I realize now that when I tell you too much information, you just can't hear me.*

"I definitely heard you! The problem is that I don't understand you!" *I will leave you very soon if you don't do what I say.* Martin was silent. *First silence your thoughts. They are erupting constantly.* Martin did as he was told. *Now here is the hard part. Change your confusion of me into knowledge of me.*

Feel as if because you don't know you understand all the better. Common sense is irrelevant. No perceivable words can describe what you're supposed to be doing. Just try.

Martin focused as the copy directed. Eventually he stopped thinking and focusing and started to just try and know. Nothing seemed to work. He wasn't giving up. He tried again and again and again. Time seemed to simply not work but then again, he was asleep. Or at least he thought he was. After some time of this, he felt a tiny gleam in the back of his head. Instead of going to it, he willed it to him.

His copy was right; there were no words for what he was supposed to do. He felt somehow, there was something in between knowledge and understanding and yet it was also in between not knowing and thinking. And if they were all interlocked, which they were and weren't, then it was in between that as well. It was both a place and a way of thinking and so many other things that couldn't be described. And he had just learned how to do it.

The Power of Hatred

12

Fillip sat by the tree, shivering in the cold as Dan, Martin and Jess slept peacefully. Naturally, he couldn't get any sleep for fear of meeting that copy of his, or meeting some raging beast that would see his sleeping figure as some kind of after-meal snack. He was angry at his confusion and helplessness. His mind was in turmoil with thoughts and fears. He had had a headache since they had talked about their copies. They weren't even supposed to have any copies, thanks to that device that Grey had given them. **I hate Grey!** He thought to himself.

"Oh, do you?" a voice said from behind Fillip. He recognized that voice. As he spun around, to his surprise, he not only saw Grey, but he also saw Black and White. He glanced up and gave Grey the most piercing look he could muster. Grey easily responded to this with a shrug and a casual, yet exasperated look. "Now, my little gizmo had done its job, and it has done it spectacularly at that."

Fillip suddenly found himself shivering as he realized that he might have irritated one of the beings that helped create power and destruction. Then Grey smiled his so-joyful-and-so-untrustworthy smile and said, "I would tell you what's going on, but that really isn't me at all."

"What good can you do anyway?" Fillip asked, and then knew that it was the wrong thing to say.

Grey just smiled. Then as quick as lightning he waved his hand and the forest that they had passed through earlier now erupted in flames. The flames were no different color than they were back where Fillip came from, red, orange, gleaming colors of heat that broke Fillip down to shaking uncontrollable in fear.

"Oh dear! Sorry about that!" Grey said. He started to chuckle as the forest seemed to scream in agony. Fillip tried to get up and run but he seemed to be stuck in place. Without hesitation, Black and White both shot out streams of blue light that wrapped around Grey and held him frozen in place. There was still a grey fog around him, but he seemed to stop moving entirely. Then White seemed to douse the fire abruptly and completely with a spray of white light. The night became still and quiet again and Fillip found that he could move. He stopped shaking. The blue spray around Grey gradually faded away but by that time Grey had calmed down. "What are you doing here anyway?" Fillip asked.

"Well," White began, "We were sent here to see if you knew what was going on and if you have found a way to get out. We also came to find out if you know what's going on in the bigger sense. I would help explain things to you, but Black will only try and stop me. We should work together as much as possible at least for the sake of the High Force." All the same, Fillip saw the look of loathing when White glanced at Black. At once Fillip wanted to change the subject.

"Wouldn't Grey be on Black's side if destruction is, at least in my mind, a bad thing?" Fillip asked. White sighed. The interaction between the three entities was a confusing subject.

"No," White said with a tone of voice that said that she was very glad indeed that it was not so. White continued, "You see, the destruction of a bad thing can sometimes be a very good thing indeed. We didn't create goodness, badness, and destruction; we were just made because they exist. I'm not sure if I can explain it well enough for you." Fillip, feeling very brave, got enough courage to ask,

"I think that White is the best because I think that goodness and happiness is the best, and White seems to be the most involved with me. But, there are many people that think of evil as being a good thing. Does Black get most involved with them?" This time Black spoke,

"No. You see, we are only these colors to you because you find what White fights for is the good thing and so that is what your White is. There is actually no good side or bad side; it's just how you look at it. If you thought that destruction is good, then Grey would be your White and both White and I would be your Grey and Black. Right now you are fighting for what your White fights for…But, just because your White fights for it now, that doesn't mean that it's the right thing to fight for."

Fillip thought about that for a moment. Then White spoke, gently and quietly,

"I'm afraid that's all that we can say now. Good luck." Then all three of them disappeared. Fillip wondered what they had meant by "the bigger sense". If there is something that Black, White, and Grey were confused about, it must a tremendously big problem, Fillip thought. But the thing that concerned him most of all was that glance of hate that they had passed each other. If serious conflict ever broke lose between the forces that helped create good, power and destruction, what would happen to everything else?

The Second View

13

Dan found himself in the place he wanted to be the very least of all. He was in that forest place again, but this time he didn't have to go down any path to find himself face to face with his copy. **"Hello. I would like to know what you meant the last time I talked to you."**

Oh, that. Well you see, it did make sense in some form. Either you just weren't consciously aware that I was making any sense, or you may have understood but not actually remembered what it was that you understood. Or maybe you did understand me, and it did make sense, but before receiving it, you categorized it as a dream that doesn't make any sense at all. In any case, I'll do what I can to make sense to you this time. You had better learn quickly or I won't get to explain it to you at all, understand?

Dan felt quite annoyed, but he contained it and said, **"Who are you?"** *You would know the answer to that question, but I actually knew you before you knew* *me, before you could think. I am you. I can make you very happy or very sad. I live off your emotions really, and here, emotions can be much more powerful than anywhere else.*

Dan was sure he understood then. "**So you're my subconscious.**" His copy clapped his hands trying to look very serious. *Very good.*

"**And do you control everything around here? Is it your game? Are we your game? Just tell me this: is this place, no this dimension, is it your dimension? Are you in control here?**" *Now, now, let's not be too harsh about it, I'm only doing what I was made to do.*

"**It's really a simple question. Is that how it works here?**" There was a short pause. *In a way. But in getting you here, I didn't do anything at all, that would require something much greater than just your subconscious. All I do is completely irrational work. At least that's what I did until we got here. Now things are different. I'm afraid that without MindLite you can't really talk to me for very long or very well. That's it for now. Goodbye.*

"Wait! What's MindLite?" And then everything in the scene around him dissolved and Dan woke up, finding himself lying on the ground where they had stopped to rest.

Martin woke up with a start and a bit of regret that he hadn't gotten the chance to talk more to his copy, but at least before the dream finished he had learned what he would have to do next time he saw his copy. That was a relief. He got up and found that Dan, Fillip and Jess were talking a few yards away. They were staring at the forest they had crossed the night before. It looked like there had been some kind of wildfire that had recently been put out. Some of the trees had burned down, but many of them were just blackened. It was as if the fire had been put out abruptly.

Martin went over to them. Fillip then told Martin about what had happened with White, Black and Grey the night before and all Martin could do was sit down, visibly shaken. They then all sat and each told of their experiences the previous night.

Fillip was practically smoking with envy. He had wanted to understand what was happening most of all, but that only made him realize that there was even more he did not know. On the other hand, Martin and Dan didn't seem to have any problem at all. They didn't get upset about all the mysteries that were happening to them. And they were the ones who were getting one step closer to solving their predicament. It wasn't fair! What was the lesson he was supposed to be learning?

Once Fillip had calmed down, he realized that the reason he was so frustrated was that he had a fair amount of control over his life back home, but now he wasn't in control at all. And he clearly didn't understand what was going on. Maybe if he had realized that sooner, he would be the one telling Martin and Dan what information he had. He decided that he would need to go along with the flow until he knew how to handle it. All he could do now was to wait and to do whatever he could to grasp what was going on. He did feel important because it was him that the spirits had come to talk to, not Dan or Martin. And tonight, he was going to meet with his copy. Then something popped up in the back of his mind that he had been wondering for a while now.

"Dad," Fillip said, "Why did you set off the warp anyway?" Martin sighed. Now it was unavoidable. He would just have to tell them. So he told them how he was trying to go to the fourth dimension because of the cry of help from his friends. He also told them how he had made a mistake and how it had brought them to the fifth dimension. Maybe in a way, this mistake would turn out to be a good thing after all. It was, in a way, amusing that it had been them, of all people, to make a mistake and discover the fifth dimension.

Fillip and Dan were silent. Martin was glad that they weren't angry at him for making this mistake and also for not planning to bring them along with him. Fillip got up. Martin, Dan and Jess followed suit after they realized that he wasn't just stretching.

"Let's go," said Fillip.

"Where?" asked Dan. Fillip spun around in a circle a few times, and then stopped.

"That way," he said, pointing to a hill in the distance. They began walking in that direction, taking breaks every once and a while. They didn't talk very much; all of them were mostly just thinking. Thinking about what was happening, what was going to happen, and mostly, what had already happened. Martin and Dan watched as Fillip led the way, determined to find something or to do something that would help somehow. Then, suddenly, everything went black for Martin and Dan, as if someone had shut off their vision with a switch.

Fillip had been walking for quite a while, not even looking back at the other two, when he heard a voice. Fillip spun around. What he saw scared him. There was a kid, about a year older that Fillip and close to his size. He was wearing jeans and a white shirt and his nails were long and dirty. He had some sort of a pack on his back, and his lips were very chapped. He was skinny and bony and his eyes were red and bloodshot, so that the whites of his eyes were not clearly visible. He had a wide toothy grin, showing yellow teeth, quite a few of which were missing. Fillip thought he looked mad, yet he had a terrible, scary smile.

"Hi," the boy said. He took a few steps closer to Fillip and Fillip quickly took many steps backwards, bumping into a tree. Fillip started when he looked around and realized that Martin and Dan were not in sight.

"My name is Jace. What is yours?" he said, quite calmly. Before Fillip had a chance to answer, he then screamed, "AND WHAT ARE YOU DOING HERE! You were never invited, you and your warp. THIS IS MY DIMENSION, AND YOU ARE NOT WELCOME HERE! NOR IS ANYONE ELSE. You should be thanking me that I let you have the 3rd dimension, but NO! You go off and start living in my other dimension! You will pay, as did those others...!"

The boy's eyes suddenly bulged and yellow veins could be seen. The roots of the tree that Fillip had backed into started moving. They slowly wrapped around Fillip's feet and sank into the ground. "I see that this dimension does not like you either," the boy said. Branches started wrapping around Fillip as well, holding him tightly to the tree. A sickening feeling rose in the back of his throat. He realized that this had happened to him before, quite a long time ago. It had happened in a nightmare.

"Take him to the house," the boy said to the tree, as if Fillip couldn't hear him. Fillip then remembered that in his nightmare, the rocks nearby had lifted off the ground and flung themselves at him, but right before they had hit him, his dream had ended, and he had awakened. This time the nightmare did not end. The rocks rose up in the air and flew at him, hard. Everything went black.

Alone

14

Jess was worried. Upon waking up this morning, no one had really noticed her. They each had told their stories and then Fillip had left. Jess didn't even get a chance to tell them what had happened to her last night, her dream. In her dream there was a fire, and a boy stepped out of the flames. Fillip ran away from the boy but then suddenly stopped. The boy said that his name was Jace. The next moment Martin and Dan disappeared and Jess saw Jace and Fillip walking towards a house. There was a holographic timepiece floating outside the house and it had a face that was laughing. Jess saw the boy talking to Fillip, who was lying on the floor of a room, crying. There were others in the room, and they were all screaming, "Help!" Then Jess saw Mathonog. He was walking toward her with a horrible smile on his face. In his hand was an electronic screwdriver, identical to the one that had almost destroyed her one year ago.

Jess had awakened before Mathonog had reached her. She was thinking so hard about her dream that she hadn't said anything to the others. Dreams were new things for her; she had never had them until the previous week. Martin said that the more Jess stayed with them the more she started taking on the characteristics of human beings. Jess believed that this was much better than anything Mathonog and Soseph had planned for her when they had created her in their laboratory. She didn't care how much more advanced the Xalpons were than humans; she still found them much crueler, all of them. Whatever had gotten better for them while evolving in the sixth dimension, other things had surely gotten worse.

Jess hated them. They had given her a brain, and yet made her for experimentation. They had tried to destroy her in order to find a substance in her that might help them do whatever they felt like doing. Apparently right now they felt like killing Martin. Jess personally didn't think anyone or anything stood a chance against those two, but she planned to do everything in her power to help Martin.

Jess had then followed Martin, Fillip, and Dan through the forest silently, thinking about her dream and what it could mean, if it meant anything at all. But, considering recent events, she wouldn't be at all surprised if it meant something. She was suddenly jolted out of her trance when she flew right into the branches of a tree. She spun around, and realized that Martin, Fillip and Dan were nowhere in sight.

Then Jess heard the voice of a boy off in the distance. She still couldn't see anyone, so she followed the voice. As Jess flew closer she heard other noises. First, she heard a loud noise that sounded like a tree falling over. Then there was the sound of someone going through a warp, and all the noises stopped. The quiet was so great it was ringing in Jess' ears, and she strained hard to hear any of the sounds that were so loud and clear a few seconds ago. She heard nothing.

"Martin? Dan? Fillip!" she said in the loudest voice she could muster. She was never programmed to yell because obviously no one saw any need in teaching her. Jess struggled with her rising panic. She was alone.

Mourndess stared at the woman for a few seconds before saying,

"Hi, I'm Rewortan." She decided that just in case it would be better not to tell anyone here her name. "Nice to meet you," she put out her hand. She smiled as Yargentia shook her hand and said,

"Let me show you around." As Yargentia walked around, showing Mourndess the places that would be important to her here...if she were to stay. Of course after what Mathonog and Soseph had done to her, she felt as if she didn't have much choice, she would have to get her revenge. She wasn't even listening to what Yargentia was saying. Instead, she was constantly looking around, searching for something to help her escape.

"Is there any...way to leave?" Mourndess said, not caring if she sounded rude.

"Well, this place is slightly different to everyone, it all depends on who you are, as does everything else that took part in the making of...everything." Mourndess realized that Yargentia often took long pauses in her sentences, as if deep in thought about whatever it was she was going to say.

"Well, tell me where your exit is and maybe I can find mine," Mourndess said. Yargentia took a quick glance at Mourndess, looking worried.

"You really don't need to go, it's very nice here, and-" Mourndess cut her off

"If by chance it was inevitable and you had to leave, where would you go?" Mourndess said, getting quite angry with this person. Yargentia said nothing for quite a while. When Mourndess thought that she wasn't going to say anything at all and turned to leave, Yargentia spoke, her voice soft this time.

"If...by chance I...had to leave...I needed to leave...or you need to leave...if I...we...we won't...we can't. There is no escape...we're stuck here. Forever." As she spoke that last word, Mourndess felt a chill running down her spine. Yargentia's head was turned in Mourndess' direction but her eyes seemed to be looking far off in the distance, as if focusing on nothing at all. Mourndess took a few startled steps back and then quickly turned and ran away.

Yargentia sighed. She supposed it made sense that no one had ever left this place. Who would really want to? But then again, she believed that no one had ever gotten here by accident, as she had. No one had a family back where they had come from; no one had a reason to leave, other than her. She couldn't say that there was truly no way out. She just knew that she had not found a way yet, and she had tried many times. Every time that she tried, something somehow would go wrong.

Yargentia had been there for four years now, and the closest she had ever gotten to leaving was a few years ago when she had someone make a pod for her. She had gotten as far as the planet's atmosphere when her ship had stopped and turned around, apparently of its own free will. It had been a starry night, without any clouds in the sky, but when she had looked out the window, instead of seeing nearby stars and planets, all she saw was a black haze. Once she had landed and gotten out, the ship had collapsed, without any warning. She had then seen a black haze come off the ship and fly away.

Yargentia remembered that day well, although sometimes it felt just like a dream to her. She missed her children so badly, and she knew that there was something out there that didn't want her to leave, that wanted to make her feel sad. Then, at times, she felt an inexplicable joy and happiness that seemed to make everything okay again. The day after her ship was destroyed, she was sure that she had seen a white cloud passing overhead, and everyone other than herself seemed to forget about the incident entirely.

But Yargentia had never given up completely, and now she had found another person here who wanted to leave. If that person managed to escape somehow, then perhaps Yargentia could too. She had renewed hope.

Mathonog walked into his own laboratory. He pulled out a box that expanded to a size of a small room. It was a very convenient machine really; it was able to go to a size small enough for you to fit in your pocket and was, basically, a warp that only he could control entirely.

Mathonog and Soseph had been able to travel to many of the dimensions. They hadn't mastered all of them, but could comfortably get along in the first ten or twenty dimensions. Their warp machine could do many things in each of the dimensions, such as going to whatever time they wanted to in the fourth dimension. It could take them to any place that Mathonog and Soseph had programmed in it.

Mathonog set the warp for the closest he could get to where Martin was, although the signal they had of him was not clear. They would have to attach a proper tracer next time they found him. Occasionally the signal went very faint, or went to a different spot completely. They couldn't quite be sure if this signal was actually Martin, but there was only one way to find out: go there. So, Mathonog set the coordinates and went. There was a flash of yellow and red sparks and Mathonog got out of the warp and set it to pocket-size. He looked around. It was definitely the fifth dimension.

Martin looked around. Everything was black and white. Martin rubbed his eyes, and color started coming back. It kept on coming. Then it stopped. Everything looked very dream-like. Color had returned, but not nearly as colorful as it had been. Everything looked dull and blurry. Martin saw that everything looked otherwise the same as before. He knew he was still in the fifth dimension. Martin pinched himself, hard. No pain. He waited a few seconds. Then, the pain of his pinch gradually appeared. It was definitely not like what it was like when he was awake. He decided that the only reasonable explanation was that he was both awake and asleep.

As Martin looked at the sky, everything blurred out of view and he saw a boy, sitting alone on a dirt path. He was about four years old, Martin assumed. It was raining heavily, but the boy did not cry. He was holding a teddy bear, a ragged and torn teddy bear. The boy was holding the bear in a tight hug, looking around him with no sign of sadness, just curiosity. He seemed happy enough, but Martin felt the strong urge to run over there and comfort him, but Martin could not move.

Suddenly, the image wavered and disappeared, showing Grey. Grey did not seem happy. His usual smug grin was not on his face. He showed only pure hatred and anger. Martin had never seen him that way, and was frightened by the image of Grey enraged so.

Then, Grey's face seemed to lighten up slightly, and his grin starting to come back.

"Jace." Grey said the words that echoed many times and brought a shiver down Martin's spine. Martin saw the boy again, sitting in the mud. Grey's words then echoed once more and it seemed that the boy heard them. Then the boy started to change; he was angry. His eyes started getting red. Veins started popping out of his neck. His muscles started to bulge.

The boy then looked at his teddy bear, waited a few seconds, then shredded it and dropped it in the mud. A small grin started on his face, similar to that of Grey's. The boy got up and started to walk away. The image faded out of view and Martin was brought back to his blurred reality. Martin shivered once more, and then he started to take a look around, trying to find Dan, Fillip, anyone, although a small thought in the back of his mind told him that he did not want to meet that boy, ever.

MindLite

15

Fillip had the strangest dream. He started to wake up slowly, then consciousness rushed in and he sat up sweating. Or at least he tried to get up, but he was actually tied tightly against a particularly thick tree branch, which happened to be moving. It wasn't a dream after all. The tree was moving toward a small shack-like structure. Fillip saw out of the corner of his eye that Jace was there too. Just then, Jace saw Fillip awake and said,

"So, you're awake already? You'll be staying here tonight." The boy indicated to the shack. "You will be heavily guarded so I suggest that you don't even attempt to escape. Tomorrow morning I'll bring you to the dimension warp, and I'll take you to my house. I hope you will be comfortable there, because," he said with a broad grin, "You will never leave." Fillip thought over these words a little while, and then shivered.

"This can't be real," Fillip practically pleaded with the boy to agree with him. "This must be magic."

Fillip said this while looking at the tree that was currently taking him to the house.

"No," Jace said and, after a short pause, "But at times, reality can be magical." Fillip thought of these words as he was taken from the tree and brought into the shabbiest room in the shack, and the door closed behind him. He thought of those words for a long time after he had been left in that room, until sleep finally came to his troubled mind.

As he slipped into a dream world, Fillip found himself in the forest area and he could see his copy. He remembered Martin's words. He remembered exactly how Martin had described talking to his subconscious mind. He felt the feeling Martin had felt, as Martin had said, words could not described it! He reached for the feeling. First physically, but when he found that this didn't work, he just felt it, knew it. Then he tried just understanding MindLite for what it was. Somewhere in his mind he saw it, mentally; he reached towards it, and it came suddenly. It rushed towards him and he was alone with his copy. Everything in every direction was just blank, less color than even white, or black. *Congratulations.*

"Did I do it?" *Yes, you did better than expected, but it was naturally easier for you anyway.*

"How?" *Well, you see, generally, younger people are closer to the time when the mind is still developing, and constantly the subconscious mind is put to use. Most people lose that close connection when they get older, although some keep it fairly strong. Also, some kids, like you, have another advantage: their imagination, a very, very powerful thing, is always here.* Fillip felt great joy at knowing that he was succeeding in this difficult task.

"Can you tell me what's going on?" *Yes. As far as my knowledge reaches, but I see what is probable, what subconsciously you noticed. What I see may not always be true, but my ability to tell what is likely is stronger here. Ask me what you need to know and I will do my best.*

"Can't you tell what I'm thinking?" *No, I can't tell what consciously you are thinking, but I can feel emotional changes and stress and bewilderment and so I'll do what I can to help.*

"So, this is MindLite?" *That's what it's called.*

"And this is the dimension of the subconscious?" *This is generally called the 5ᵗʰ dimension, but it is also known as the dimension of the subconscious.*

"What is special about this dimension? How is it different than the 3ʳᵈ dimension? How did Jace manage to control those inanimate objects? Can I? What happened to Martin and Dan? Why? Where is Jess? Are any of them in danger? Is there something I can do here to help us in any way? Where is our warp? Is there any other way to escape the 5ᵗʰ dimension? Where are Mathonog and Soseph? What are they doing? Who is Jace? Why is he after us? Why does he think that all the dimensions are his? Where are Black, White, and Grey? What is going on?"

Fillip fired question after question, not even stopping for an answer. He was glad to vent his frustration. His last question seemed to echo for a long time.

"I'm afraid." *I know.*

Fillip already knew that his copy understood his fear, but it did not make the fear go away. Yet knowing that someone understood, even if it was actually a part of him, made Fillip fell a little better. There was plenty of time to get all his questions answered because he knew that he would stay asleep for a long time.

I'll answer what I can. Are you ready? Fillip nodded, he was ready. His subconscious began.

Mathonog looked at his scan. Martin should be somewhere near, he thought. His radar showed no activity. Maybe Martin had left. Mathonog started a complete multidimensional scan, annoyed that it would take about 30 parsecs. The radar reported to him that in a search of all the known dimension, Martin was absolutely nowhere to be found. Frustrated, Mathonog decided to look around his current location. Maybe the radar was malfunctioning.

Mathanog scanned slowly, searching everywhere. Maybe he could find one of the Martin's sons and maybe they could tell him where Martin was. He didn't want to go all the way across the dimension just to find that his radar was wrong. He thought that there might not be anyone here and that he should turn around and go back. He would tell Soseph that he could not find them, and that they should try again later.

Suddenly Mathonog had an idea. Maybe, there was an explanation to why his scan could not locate Martin. His idea explained why Martin had disappeared from his screen and couldn't be found anywhere. It was a simple explanation really. And it meant that Mathonog's troubles would be over. Martin must be dead.

A Ruined Plan

16

Even though Mathonog did not have the pleasure of bringing about Martin's end, it came, just as planned. He didn't care that he hadn't killed Martin, but Soseph didn't have to know that. Who knows? Maybe Soseph would even praise him for getting the job done so quickly. Everything had been settled. Mourndess, still floating around in a shuttle, was very far away, and Martin was dead. All they had to do now was to find the Shattering Device and then, their goal would finally be achieved. After all this time, it all had gone as he had planned.

Selfish thoughts rose into his mind as he wondered if he would even tell Soseph that Martin had been killed. All he had to do was return to his home and find the Shattering Device. Then, finally, he would have it. All to himself. But there was a generous side of him, one he didn't even know he had. He would tell Soseph. He would tell him everything, until the final moment would come, and then he would complete his quest alone. The power was meant for him alone. He was sure of it.

Jess, now frantic, was flying around wildly, calling out the names of her lost friends, even though she was almost positive that she wouldn't find anyone. Just as she was thinking this, she flew over two people. She stopped, turned around, and flew back, slower this time, and looked down. There, lying on the ground, were Dan and Martin. Worried, she flew over, and with one of her sensitive feelers, she felt their pulses. They were sleeping.

"Sleeping! You're sleeping! How can you be sleeping! Where's Fillip? Don't tell me he's sleeping too. Where should I look, a bush?" But neither Martin nor Dan responded, or even stirred, for that matter. Jess was frantic. She touched them again, on the backs, with her feelers extremely hot, hot enough to burn. She held it there for a few seconds, but neither Martin nor Dan even shifted. Nothing she tried worked. She flew closer to try other ways to wake them when she heard,

"It's not going to work." Jess turned around and saw Martin. There lying on the ground was Martin, there standing in front of her was Martin. She suddenly realized what must be going on; the Martin standing in front of her must be the one that Martin meets in his dreams, his subconscious, or his copy.

"Why not?" Jess demanded.

"He's trapped in his sleep, and so is Dan. The only way to wake him is to use a device that a boy here has. His name is Jace. I can't tell exactly where he is, but a tree followed him, whose tracks will be very easy to follow."

"Sorry. Did you say a tree followed him?"

"A tree." He said it slowly this time, enunciating. There was no mistaking it. Then the copy of Martin disappeared. Jess turned around and decided she must start looking for a tree that had just walked away.

Mathonog took out his teleporter box and just as he was going to teleport home, something flew by, slowly. Mathonog hid behind a tree as it passed by. He peeked out from the side of the tree to see if he could identify what it was. He didn't believe his eyes. It was Jess. He saw that she was mumbling something to herself.

"Okay, so I need to get to that device, then Martin and Dan can wake up from their sleep, and then we are going to have to find Fillip. I wonder who that Jace is anyway, and why he did that to Dan and Martin. I wonder what got him so mad. Maybe Fillip will be found somewhere near that guy..."

She went on, but Mathonog wasn't listening anymore; he understood now. Some person named Jace has some device that put Martin into a deep sleep, so deep that Martin did not register on his scan. He wasn't dead. But where was he? Jess needed to find this device and turn off the controls, because she wanted to wake up Martin and Dan. Then Martin would register on his scan and he could find him.

Jess was Mathonog's creation and maybe his most valuable one too. He desired to get her so that he could take her apart, scan the materials and get more of them. She had already proven more than once how useful she was. But he needed Jess alive to take Martin out of his sleep so that he could find him and kill him. Then he could take Jess.

Maybe he could just find Jace himself and set off his device, but he didn't know who Jace was. Jace certainly didn't mean to treat Martin and his family very well, so maybe he would be on Mathonog's side. But he was probably a person not to be trusted. It was Mathonog's chance to prove his worth and he wasn't going to mess it up. He just needed a plan. None of his ideas seemed workable. For the first time in his life Mathonog didn't know what to do.

The Planet with No Escape

17

Mourndess kept running, bumping into an alien, until she couldn't run any more. She wouldn't believe it. She couldn't believe it. There had to be some escape. She was angry. She had been sent in a pod so that she would never return and never foil Mathonog and Soseph's plans. By amazing chance, she had been sent here, and freed from her pod torture, only to find that she couldn't leave. She felt like this could not be happening, and that Yargentia must be wrong. She tried a friendly looking alien, a small, fat, red, creature with eyes instead of hands on two thin flexible arms and six other thick burly arms, each with hands with six fingers.

"Is there any way to leave this planet, this place?" she asked, politely. With a low voice he said,

"Well, I don't see why you would want to leave, but yes it is possible…but not yet. I am currently making a pod for a special occasion. I'm still not sure it will actually work. If it works for me, then I could make you one, though it would take a year or two."

"No, just curious, is there any other way to leave?"

"No, many have looked a long time for one. Haven't found it yet if there is one."

"What's your name?"

"Pallk. I live over there." He pointed to a very small hut.

"Goodbye."

"Goodbye." Mourndess knew what she would have to do. She would wait until Pallk was done making that pod. Then she would steal it. And leave. And find Mathonog and Soseph. And ruin their plans. And get the Shattering Device once and for all.

Plans

_18_

Jess wandered aimlessly, not sure exactly how to look for a tree that wasn't there any more. As a matter of fact, she did hear the occasional rustle of a bush, or the cracking noise of leaves being broken under someone's feet, but each time she heard this, she would turn around and see nothing. Well, it can't be too hard, she thought sarcastically. All I have to do is find somewhere where a tree decided that it didn't want to be anymore and left, then I can follow its tracks, and there lying on a golden platter for all to see, will be some device with a switch that will turn everything back to the way it was and make everything right. Hey, maybe I could ask a bush...thoughts tumbled through her mind as she passed over a spot where there was a large crater in the ground, where something the shape of a tree, roots and all, had been uprooted.

Mathonog had finally decided on a plan. He would follow Jess, hide, and then as she was finding the switch, he would help her by finding Jace and distracting him. He wouldn't tell Jace everything, but mainly let him talk until he could sum up whether Jace was on his side or not. If he was on his side, then they could work something out, maybe he could even give the others to Jace, as long as he got Martin. Now, if Jace was not on his side, then he could easily make an escape with one of his many devices. There would be no need to kill Jace, because if he took Fillip and Dan out of the way, he really would be helping him after all.

Then he could find Martin and kill him. How hard could that be? After that, he could take Jess back to his laboratory and leave the others for Jace. Perfect. Or so he hoped.

As soon as Dan came to, he saw the exact same thing that Martin did. He looked around; everything was a slightly blurry and not very colored version of the fifth dimension. He tried to talk, but no noise came out. After a while of searching in a forest similar to the one that he, Martin, Fillip, and Jess were in earlier, he found that when he walked into a tree, he went straight through it. Then, he stopped very suddenly. There, lying on the ground he saw himself and Martin. He looked down closer and saw, to his relief, that both of them were breathing, ever so slightly. He thought about this for quite a while. Then, he thought, this must be a dream, right? He pinched himself. No pain came. He pinched himself again, much harder, still no pain. That was it then, he was asleep.

Dan sat down and waited for something to happen. He waited a long time, he couldn't tell how long he waited, maybe hours, maybe minutes, or maybe even days. He expected at any minute, maybe a spaceship would come and crash right on him, and right before it hit him he would wake up, or something similar to that. After a while, he realized that this wasn't happening, and this dream suddenly changed to a nightmare. He couldn't wake up, he couldn't escape. When he was younger, he had a nightmare every night for years. He slowly learned a tactic for him that brought him out of his sleep. No matter what danger lay ahead of him, he would just stay still, blink and will himself to escape. It always worked for him. It always let him escape. And he knew it would be the only thing that would get him out of here. He stayed perfectly still and suddenly, almost surprising himself; he blinked and forced himself out of his dream. He opened his eyes. He was still in the dream.

Questions

19

So, let's do this one question at a time, and remember that I'm not all-knowing. I've just got a slightly deeper understanding of what's going on than you do. Now, to the questions. This dimension is special because the ground is constantly soaking in knowledge, knowledge that we, the subconscious, can gain. This dimension is massively large because none of it exists in the physical plane. It exists only in the mental plane.

Everything around you was created by a thought, a set up for a dream. Usually, you can only see your own thoughts, but the dimensions are overlapping more than they ever have before, and even your dimension is overlapping with the fifth. That means that inhabitants of your dimensions could have dreams that come to be here, or worse, you, Martin, Dan, and Jess could create someone else's dream without trying to.

The dimensions are expanding and no one really knows why. While almost all other dimensions are mostly physical and spatial, like yours, the fifth is much more psychological, which is why the impossible is really quite natural. Jace animated that tree because this dimension knows him and he knows the dimension. With practice you probably could animate an inanimate object, but it is very difficult to do correctly. If something goes wrong and you don't create the object perfectly, it could do whatever it please. Sometimes, made up beings such as the tree, can be much more powerful than physical beings and can do horrible things. It would probably take several years of practice to make it perfect.

"Well then how does Jace do it?" There was a short pause. *I don't know. Jace did something to Martin and Dan, I don't know what but it made them unable to move, lost in sleep. Jace has incredible powers. I believe that Jess is coming to try to save them.*

"Will she find me?" *Probably not. You will probably be somewhere else by the time she reaches us; Jace said we will be leaving here tomorrow morning. In answer to the question whether any of them are in danger, yes. We're all in danger here at all times. And* *whether there is something you can do here to help any of them, I don't know. Your best chance would be to get as much information as you possibly can. You may be able to think of something at the time.*

As for Mathonog and Soseph, one of them may currently be here. I think that they still seek Martin and by now they have probably found him. I think that Jace currently has your warp because he knows everything that goes on around here. I really don't know why Jace is after you, but I know that he believes that all the dimensions are his. I have a feeling that someday we are going to find out why he believes that. Maybe you will be able to figure it out soon.

I don't know where White, Black, and Grey are but it seems as if they are doing a lot of things right now. Something is going wrong, different from how they thought it would be. The dimensions are overlapping and expanding more than they have ever before, and they think that it is a bad sign. They are trying to figure out what has gone wrong. Power is found in all of the least expected places in the dimensions, and Black, White, and Grey all seem to be expecting something. They are waiting.

Part Two:

Return to the Fourth Dimension

The Talk

20

Once Jess had found the tree's track, the sun was already starting to set, making it more difficult to see. As the sun shed less and less light on the forest, Jess turned on her laser vision and moved slowly, making sure she was following the right tracks. Mathonog followed slowly behind Jess. Jess followed the tracks straight throughout the night. After sunrise she and Mathonog were still following them. Jess suddenly stopped. There, where the tracks stopped, was a tree. It was a normal tree. Jess went around to the back of it and she saw a very large shack. She had found Jace's place.

Fillip was taken just as the sun rose. He didn't struggle at all. Jace walked him to a booth with a white and blue warp inside and he was transported somewhere, with red and yellow sparks following him. Then he was in a stone cell, with metal bars and an electronic security system. It was clearly a prison of sorts, with a toilet and a bed. Fillip supposed that this was "his house" as Jace had called it. He was not sure what dimension he was in.

Jess was actually very strong for a bug of her size, and could open doors if she had to. She would put two feelers on the doorknob and get them to stick, and then she would fly in the direction to turn it. After turning the knob, she would fly backwards with her body under the doorknob, and pull the door open. She did that now. Mathonog watched with fascination. When Jess flew in, Mathonog followed slowly and silently. He watched as Jess flew into one room.

It was a big room, full of papers and devices, but not Jace. Hopefully, Jess would find the switch here. He checked two other rooms before he found Jace. Jace was in a very comfortable room with biochairs and aerial loungers. There was a biochair with its back to the doorway, and a boy relaxing in it. Before Mathonog got the chance to say anything, the boy spoke.

"Hello," he said. The chair spun around. Mathonog quickly but silently closed the door, so that Jess would not hear. Then he faced the boy.

"Hello, Jace." To his immediate displeasure, Mathonog found that his voice was hoarse, showing his true fear of the boy.

"What, exactly, are you doing here?" Jace asked. The boy showed no fear of him. He knew that Mathonog was dangerous and yet knew that he himself was even more so.

"Well," Mathonog began, selecting his words carefully. "I have learned that we have visitors to the fifth dimension, and that is unacceptable. I came here to bring them back. I could help you, in one small way. Martin and an electronic beetle that you may not have found yet…I would like to have the honor of killing them myself."

The boy thought about this for a few seconds. "Where is that beetle now?" the boy asked. Mathonog gulped. He hadn't planned for that.

"I don't know, but if you or I ever find it, may I have it?"

"If I find it, I suppose you may have it, but I want you to know that I'm not siding with you and we have completely different thoughts, about everything."

"Yes, of course. And Martin? He has caused multiple problems for me and it would be very kind if-"

"First of all, I know that you live in the fourth dimension and I have accepted that. You and your friend are different than those humans."

"Thank you."

"Second of all I want you to know that I know what you really came here for, but will let you live because currently our desires are similar." Mathonog shuddered.

"I will kill Martin," Jace said. Mathonog realized that it really didn't make a difference whether he or Jace killed Martin. As long as he could be sure that it would be done.

"It's a deal," Mathonog said and put out his hand for Jace. Just as Jace was about to stand up, suddenly swirls of white and black appeared on either side of him. Then a blue haze surrounded him, freezing him in his tracks. Mathonog stood there for a few seconds, then seized the moment and ran out the door. He looked around; Jess was still in the room, with the door closed behind her. Mathonog ran out of the shack and found his tracks back where he came, following them at full-speed.

Ruined Again

21

As soon as Jess entered the room she started to look around. There were many things in the room, and she would have to look through all of them. So, she got started. She looked around the room at all the devices she found, and examined them all. Behind a large dimension air-sketch for an invention, she saw a storeroom. She wondered where Jace had gotten all these things, or the money to obtain them.

She looked through the storeroom and found a small warp. Next to it was a translucent apparatus with a control on it. After close examination she realized that this was the deep sleep machine. Jess extended her feelers so that she could put the warp on her back, and the feelers could hold it there. As she was about to grab the apparatus, she was knocked sideways and sent flying. It was one of the black leather-like creatures that Martin had used in his escape from Mathonog and Soseph's place the year before. Jess wondered how they could have gotten here, and then realized that one of her first nightmares had been about these creatures.

Jess sent a beam of searing heat the creature's way, and the creature yelled in pain, stumbling backwards. Jess quickly grabbed the apparatus, and flew as fast as she could, balancing both devices carefully on her back. She didn't need to look where she was going, because her memory banks remembered the exact path she had taken the night before and she flew fast, fast enough so that everything around her was a blur.

After reaching the spot where he had discovered Jess the day before, Mathonog searched frantically for Martin. After a few minutes of searching, he found Martin and Dan, lying on the ground. They were still in their deep sleep. Mathonog got out a lethal ionic gun. He grinned. All of his troubles had finally ended. He pointed the gun at Martin. Finally, he could...His thought was interrupted by a searing burning pain in his wrist. He dropped the ionic gun. There was Jess. She deactivated the apparatus and immediately Martin and Dan were awake, as wide-awake as ever.

"What is going...?" Dan started, but was interrupted when Jess yelled,

"Run, now!" Without question, they did as they were told. After a few seconds of running as hard as they could, Jess turned around while still flying backwards. Mathonog was nowhere in sight. She flew backwards into a tree, thus activating the controls on the warp attached to her back. The warp appeared, surrounding Martin, Dan, and Jess, and sending them flying out of the fifth dimension. Mathonog, who had realized what was happening, was running after them.

"No!" he cried out loud. It couldn't be possible. They had escaped him. Everything was going according to plan and yet they managed to escape him. Still not believing this was possible, Mathonog ran on. Then he stopped. He looked around. He couldn't believe his eyes. All around him, there were yellow and red sparks. They had left. Martin, Dan, and Jess had been flung back to the third dimension. Without Fillip.

Jace woke up from his trance and saw that Mathonog had left. He checked his scanner and saw that Martin and Dan were no longer in the fifth dimension.

Someone must have used his device and woken them from their sleep. He got up. He went to his Connector and created a warp for the fourth dimension. Jace decided that it was time to visit his prisoner.

The House

_22_

Fillip felt strange feelings in his prison cell. In a way, he felt that he must be guilty, because he was in prison, even though it wasn't the type of prison that he would be locked in for committing a crime. In any case, he felt guilty that he had failed and had gotten caught. He was overwhelmed by feelings of pain, guilt, anger and sadness swelling in the chest, making it difficult to breathe, but at the same time he didn't care. It was as if nothing mattered. No energy ran inside him.

He didn't feel hunger and ate little that day, even though he got one meal a day. He barely moved, sinking lower into his cell. When Jace returned that night with a robotic guard to take back Fillip's food bowl, he looked down and saw how little of the contents had been eaten. He looked up at Fillip.

"Still eating?" Jace asked. Fillip didn't respond, but just stared at Jace, hatred burning in his eyes. Jace smiled and chuckled as he then gave it to one of the robots who took it, looked at it, then ate it madly, a mess of food everywhere.   Jace chuckled again and said,

"Are you sure you don't want to eat that?" Still grinning, he and his guards left the cell to Fillip. Fillip sat like that the entire night, still not moving. He was tired, but too lazy to enter his small bed with no pillow or covers. He did not sleep at all. There was no window, so it was impossible to tell what time it was. When Fillip got up his legs felt weak. He collapsed and stood up again.

Fillip walked to the bed. Still refusing to think that he should have eaten his food, he fell on the bed, and, almost instantly, he fell fast into a deep dreamless sleep. He woke up much later with the screeching noise of the cell door being opened. Fillip saw that it was Jace and more robotic guards. Fillip got out of his bed and walked to the cell door and took his food. Before he could eat, Jace said,

"Your brother, father, and...electronic friend have left, returned to the third dimension." Fillip supposed that Jace was expecting this to make Fillip feel mad, and at first it did make him mad. But then, Fillip felt happiness and relief. Then he felt proud.

They had escaped the fifth dimension! They had escaped here, and found a way home! Then he was overjoyed. Happiness lived in him once more, and a wonderful feeling that he had not experienced for quite a long time returned. They had beaten them! They had won!

And with this, Fillip knew that he would too. He, too, would find a way. It was possible, he convinced himself. Strength greater than he had known he had exploded in him. Fillip felt courage like never before, down to the very marrow in his bones. Soon, he knew that he would be home talking happily with Dan and Martin, and playing at his house with Jess. And he could see his dog again. He grinned and slowly, it changed to a full smile. He stood up straight once again. Without another comment, Jace turned on his heels and walked out, his guards clumsily following behind him. Fillip stared after them in disbelief. What he was seeing couldn't be possible. Jace and his guards had left him there, with the door to the cell still wide open.

The Quite Disappointing Return

_23_

Suddenly Martin, Dan, and Jess appeared back in the third dimension. They just stood there, looking around as if they didn't recognize where they were, but they knew. They were back home, in the exact same positions that they had been before they left. The holo-timepiece told them that they had been gone for a minute or two; time wasn't the same in the other dimensions. The dog came bounding out to see them, and greeted each one like an old friend.

Actually, the only proof that they had gone anywhere at all was the fact that Fillip wasn't with them, or anywhere else in the house, or anywhere else in the planet, or in this dimension at all. None of them had any idea where he was now.

"Maybe, each of us should tell each other what happened," Dan said. "Then we can try to find Fillip."

"Okay, I'll start," Martin said. So, they each told each other exactly what happened, from when they were walking in that forest, to their dreams, to when they were running in that forest, and finally to when they were warped back to the third dimension. Jess had the most information concerning Fillip and Jace. Even after this, they really had no idea where Fillip was, and they still hadn't figured out a plan.

They also realized that they still had not rescued their friends in the fourth dimension, and didn't even know how they would find them. There had been no response on the communicator, so Martin assumed it was not in their possession any more. It did occur to Martin that the one who had taken his friends at work was Jace, and he voiced this thought. He remembered that transmission well: *We're...being...taken...there is a child...come quickly...help...*

Just the same, they realized that charging valiantly into the fourth dimension without knowing where they were, or even whether they were still in the fourth dimension, just didn't make any sense now. One thing that was clear to them was that there had been a lot of traveling between the dimensions lately. That meant that there was still a good chance that Fillip and his friends would appear here soon. If they didn't arrive soon, then Martin decided he would go back and try to find them. Martin thought the best plan would be for him to go to work and try to develop ways to protect his family and friends, and to prepare him for whatever would happen next.

Martin sat down despondent. He started to think about how his wife had disappeared four years ago. He still thought about her returning to him; he missed her so much. He was not ready at this point to lose one more person in his family. That just wasn't going to happen. Then he started to think, "How could I have made such a great mistake?" First, he traveled to the fifth dimension instead of the fourth, when his friends called him for help. Then, he came back from the fifth dimension without Fillip. Now, he wondered if he was making another mistake by not immediately going back to rescue Fillip.

The Communicator

24

Fillip walked out slowly and quietly, not daring to breathe, when he heard the sound of a large portal closing and he knew that Jace had left. Fillip took his chance, and started running as quietly as he could. First, he had to see what Jace had that would be of use to him. So he searched through the rooms, but couldn't find anything around that would be of much use. Jace probably kept things like the machine to make the robotic guards locked up somewhere.

Then, before Fillip left the last room and looked for a hiding place, his eyes caught something he hadn't seen there before. He immediately recognized it as the communicator, the one that Martin's friends at work had kept in the fourth dimension. So apparently it was Jace who had taken away the communicator! Martin's friends were probably locked up, here, in the fifth dimension!

Fillip thought that as soon as he could call home, Martin, Dan and Jess could come and rescue their friends. Fillip remembered how to make the communicator smaller, into a thin slip, and also remembered how strong it was. He tucked it into his shoe, so that nothing was showing. Then, Fillip hid in one of the storerooms and waited to see what would happen next. Fillip felt inside his shoe. The communicator inside his shoe made him feel better.

Old Enemies

25

Mathonog sat down. He sighed deeply. Maybe, we aren't who we thought we were. Maybe even if we're after you, you can survive. Maybe a human outsmarted me. But this, whether it was due to pride or fear, he couldn't take. Of course not! He wasn't going to be outsmarted by any human! He grabbed his subspace dimensional locator and it started to scan. Immediately, the locator confirmed where he thought he would find Martin: the third dimension. He smiled. He took out his warp; soon he would be seeing Martin again, and this time, Mathonog was ready.

Mathonog found himself right where he wanted to be, in the third dimension, right outside Martin's workplace. Mathonog was standing right at the entry of a very large building known as Future Discoveries. Mathonog walked in. Martin's laboratory was on the first floor. Five rooms were empty on this floor where Arnold Frizt, Lemmy Harp, Jones Walter, Jenna Gruvitz, and Marie Danica worked. They were currently studying in the fourth dimension, or so everyone but Martin believed. Many people stared at Mathonog as he walked by, because he was quite tall and had such pale eyes.

Mathonog moved towards Martin's workspace. When confronted by a security officer Mathonog took out a portable warp and sent the officer smashing right through the soft walls in that part of the building. The man landed on the ground outside. He was lucky, because the soft walls had been invented to protect those who did experiments with warps that set up magnetic fields.

The officer immediately set off the building's alarm. Mathonog walked quickly to Martin's workspace. Martin, hearing the noise and the alarm, opened up his door.

"What's happenin...?" Martin stopped talking as soon as he saw that Mathonog was standing right in front of him. Mathonog reached for his ionic gun. Martin was already carrying his own transdimensional security alarm and quickly activated it. Jess would arrive in a few minutes. Unfortunately, Martin didn't have a few minutes. He narrowly evaded the gun's deadly beams. Martin thought as quickly as he could. He saw that Mathonog was carrying an ionic gun, powered by magnified UV rays that killed instantly.

He would be killed, unless he he was protected from the rays somehow. Martin looked quickly around and found a recent invention - a spray canister packed tightly with oxygen. The oxygen was not the type that people breathed, known as O_2. Instead it contained O_3, the chemical that makes up the ozone layer that protects humans from the ultraviolet rays of the sun. Martin managed to pull on a protective gas mask that came with the ozone spray. Mathonog chuckled, as he moved around him, holding the UV gun.

Martin popped the lid on the canister and O_3 came rushing out. Mathonog shot but missed. Then Mathonog shot again, but Martin had a thick layer of ozone surrounding him. A tiny beam of UV rays scorched his back before the cloud enveloped him, and a small deep burn appeared on his back. Martin screamed but fled through the door.

Mathonog used his warp to escape, because he knew that the lungs, even of a Xalpon, could not survive breathing in all that O_3 instead of O_2. After

Martin was sure that Mathonog had gone, Martin ran back into the room and sucked the O_3 back into the canister. As soon as he was done, he sat down and sighed.

But, Mathonog appeared in the room again. He took a quick breath of air to make sure that the O_3 was gone, and then reached for his gun again. Martin didn't wait. He knocked Mathonog over and ran. He didn't notice that his communicator dropped out of his pocket and fell on the floor. He just kept on running until he saw Jess flying towards him. He felt safe.

Mathonog picked up the communicator. He supposed that Jess would be with Martin by now so he decided not to go after him. Then the device started making a low pitch, loud buzz. Mathonog put the receiver to his ears and heard Fillip's voice.

Martin! I'm in the fourth dimension! I'm in a prison with Arnold and the others! I have a lot of information and should be coming home soon! I've already started to escape! I'll tell you what happened later. Just wait for me! Is everything all right?

"Hello Fillip," Mathonog said to the device. And on the other end of the receiver, in a storeroom in a prison-like house, Fillip shuddered with fear and the communication went dead. Mathonog laughed and pocketed the communicator.

Escape?

_26_

Fillip, still shaken, felt that he needed to escape as quickly as he possibly could. When he heard the main portal open, he guessed that it was Jace and the guards. He heard the portal close and then another one opened. Once Fillip couldn't hear any more footsteps, he snuck to the main entrance and opened it just enough to slide through. Then he ran as fast as he possibly could. He had a fleeting thought that he was in the fourth dimension; this thought was confirmed when he ran straight into a warp and was sent to the other end of the fourth dimension.

Once Martin realized that he didn't have his communicator any more, he and Jess ran back to Future Discoveries and into Martin's room, where Mathonog had been waiting for Martin to return. Jess radiated enough heat so that Mathonog started to sweat and realized that Jess was there, even though his back was turned to them. Mathonog turned around, but Jess had already removed the communicator from his pocket.

Mathonog decided it was time to take his warp and leave, as Jess started to radiate heat powerful enough to kill him. Martin gladly took the communicator from Jess and turned it on. It was certainly worth a try.

"Hello?" Martin said. "Arnold, are you there?" Then he heard Fillip.

Dad! I'm here, somewhere in the fourth dimension! Come to the fourth dimension and get me out of here! Your friends are here too.

The transmission ended. Thrilled, Martin went home immediately and went to the room where they kept the Connector. He also took out a copy of the device Grey had given him to locate people who had gone through warps in the fourth dimension. He set up the warp carefully, making sure he was going to the fourth dimension. He called out for Dan to come right away.

"What is it?" Dan called.

"I found out where Fillip is."

"Where is he?"

"He's in the fourth dimension."

"Well then, let's go there!"

"That's what I'm doing. I hope you will be fine on your own..."

"What? I'm going there with you!" Dan said this so forcefully that Martin said,

"Okay." Martin and Dan stood by the Connector, initiated the activation sequence, and went through the warp side-by-side, with Jess on Martin's shoulder.

When Jace discovered that Fillip had escaped, he ran to his dimensional scanner and found exactly where Fillip was. He also learned where Martin, Dan, and Jess were. Jace took several guards and entered a warp, heading right for Martin. When Jace arrived, he and his troops immediately grabbed Martin and Dan, and he placed Jess into a deep sleep. He then surrounded them with a force field and placed them into individual warp cells. Jace was happy. Fillip may have escaped them, but now he had Martin, Dan, and Jess instead.

New Hope

27

When in their cells, Martin and Dan went by the same schedule that Fillip had when he was imprisoned. Jess was kept asleep however. Her sleep was dreamless. But neither Martin nor Dan put himself in the same position that Fillip had. They both kept their attitudes positive so that they could keep on going. Shortly after being imprisoned, Martin remembered that he still had his communicator, although Jace had taken the Locator that Grey had given him. He pulled the communicator out and was horrified to see that when Jace had tied him up, the force field had shattered it. Now he had no means of communication and, if Fillip got caught, there would be no hope for them. Fillip was their last chance, and Martin supposed that Jace would come after him any minute, if he hadn't already.

Shortly after Martin got the idea, Fillip got the same idea and tried to contact them via communicator, but when he found that it didn't work, he got worried.

What if Jace had found them? Suddenly White appeared.

"Hello," White said. "I think that you need help." Fillip just stared at her, not believing what he was hearing.

"You, you can help me?"

"Yes."

"What about Black or Grey? They won't stop you?"

"They are already starting to get involved themselves, they can't stop me."

"Why do you want to help me?"

"Because things are happening that I myself want to stop."

"Are you doing this without orders?"

"Yes, without orders." Because the only thing Fillip could see of her was a blurry ball of white, he couldn't tell, but he was almost positive he saw her smile.

"How am I going to rescue Martin, Dan, and Jess?" Fillip asked.

"That's what we're going to figure out." Now Fillip was quite sure he could see her smile.

Fillip's Rescue Attempt

28

"First of all, we need to get to Jace's house," Fillip said to White, even though he guessed that she already knew.

A warp appeared around them and there they were, standing a few yards in front of the house. Fillip smiled. It was good working with White like this. It seemed like everything was going to work out now. Then his smile disappeared. There, blocking their way into the house, were Black and Grey, along with at least 50 of Jace's robotic guards.

"What are you doing here?" White asked Black.

"I-"

"We," corrected Grey.

"Yes, we think that you are getting too involved with them," Black motioned towards Fillip.

"Me! What about him?" White pointed at Grey. Now Fillip was sure it was Black who smiled.

"I've decided that what he is doing isn't all that bad," Black said. Fillip could tell that White was furious, but he couldn't tell why.

"Fillip! Go to the door and rescue your friends! I'll protect you! Good luck!" Fillip was about to say the same for her when she said,

"Go! Now!" and he did as he was told. He ran to the door, anything in his way was flung away with white light. He reached the door and ran inside closing it behind him. Orange light covered the door, and to Fillip's luck, it locked so that no guard could break through. Now it was time to free Martin, Dan, and Jess. He would come back later and free the rest. He ran to the room with four cells in it, where he had been kept earlier.

White struggled. There were many guards, not a fair fight even if she didn't have Grey and Black to accompany them. But still she fought on, crashing into Black and Grey while slowly getting rid of the guards. She could produce an incredibly strong force field around herself, which went a long way at protecting her from harm.

Fillip found his way to the room, but once he made it there everything happened too quickly. First, Fillip saw that one cell was empty and the others had Martin, Dan, and Jess in them. Then he noticed that there, in the room with them, was Jace.

"Hello," Jace said maliciously. "Funny you should come here so quickly." He opened up the empty cell. Then Fillip saw that he had the laser keys for these four cells in his hand. He lunged for them but Jace was too quick and moved out of the way. Then Jace's expression changed.

"Please, don't hurt me," Jace said in a much higher voice than he usually spoke in.

"Give me the keys," Fillip said angrily.

"No!" Jace jumped back using his back to shield the keys.

"May I please have the keys?" Fillip said again, slowly and carefully. Jace appeared to be deep in thought.

"Okay," Jace said, and handed over the keys. Fillip stared at him, expecting him to do something bad but instead, Jace ran out, whimpering in fear. Fillip looked after him. He sure hadn't expected that to happen. He then took the keys and opened the cells that contained his brother, father and electronic friend.

Many Difficulties

29

After freeing Martin, Dan, and Jess, Fillip had to figure out how to wake Jess. He picked her up, tapped her, shook her furiously, but nothing seemed to work. He saw a little wire, coming out of a small space in her back. It was unplugged. So he plugged it back in, closed the lid, and slowly Jess's black eyes came into focus and she fluttered her wings a little bit before settling down in Fillip's hand.

After that was done, it was time to figure out how they would escape. As soon as they walked up the stairs and entered the main room, the entrance door burst open and White flew through it. Martin supposed that White, Black and Grey were all equally powerful. That meant that two against one was nearly impossible. In addition to that, all of the artificial guards had appeared to be on the side of Grey and Black as soon as they showed up, which made Martin think that White really stood no chance at all. And he couldn't forget the fact that all of them were blocking their only escape route as well. To add to this, one of the doors opened and out walked Jace, practically boiling with anger. Things were not looking good for them.

Mathonog looked at the scanner. The fourth dimension again? He was getting really tired of this. Those humans just never learn a lesson, thought Mathonog. He set his warp to teleport himself near them. He checked his coordinates so that he would come out right where Martin was. He looked it over once more, grinned, and set it off. He found himself right inside Jace's house, with Martin, Dan, Fillip, and Jess right in front of him.

Mathonog was in a really good mood, because he had just remembered to put on one of those new heat suits that completely reflect all heat far away him. He simply stepped up, tapped Martin on the shoulder, and put on the biggest grin he could manage. When Martin turned around, the color drained out of his face. Things were definitely not looking very good for Martin, Dan, Fillip, and Jess.

Martin was strained and really afraid, and felt that the situation must be hopeless now. Could White get him out of this? In comparison to Black, Grey, Jace, the guards and Mathonog, White didn't seem all that powerful anymore. Then the sounds and noises around Martin disappeared, stopped completely. He heard nothing, and everything was alien to him. Emotions flew through him, and he knew that all that noise and commotion was still happening around him, but it didn't seem to matter to him. He saw something. It was inside himself. It had been calm, waiting, but now it pushed itself to the front of his brain, and he found it and remembered, that MindLite. He felt it right now, because that is what it was, a feeling, a particularly strong feeling.

He suddenly saw his other self in front of him, and everything else disappeared. **What are you doing here? This is the fourth dimension!** *The fourth and fifth dimensions are more overlapped then ever before.* **What can I do?** Martin asked his other self, his subconscious. *Use your emotions. They exist not only to you, but to everyone else as well. Right now your subconscious is almost as powerful here as it was in the fifth dimension.* And with that he disappeared and everything returned to the way it had been, noises and commotion and all.

Martin felt all the emotions inside him, and suddenly they left him. He would never know how. He felt as if someone had freed him from a heavy burden. For a few moments Martin was emotionless, completely emotionless. It was as if his emotions had been funneled into a powerful weapon. Martin saw Mathonog standing in from of him, immobilized. Mathonog was overpowered by the magnified emotions that were taking form against him, both from Martin and from White. He couldn't think any more. All that he knew was that he needed to get away.

Mathonog managed at that point to activate his warp belt, and he was gone, back to his shuttle. Jace fell to the ground, writhing in pain. Many objects flew out of his pockets, including his stun gun and portable warp. When one apparatus flew in the air and broke, all of the robotic guards standing at the door completely disappeared from existence. Jace dragged himself up, disappeared down a passageway, and was gone. One of the items that had fallen to the ground was a set of laser keys. Fillip picked these up.

"I bet these open your friends' cells!" Fillip said excitedly to Martin. He then ran down to the lower rooms. Martin and Dan walked out to find that Grey seemed quite pleased with the havoc that Martin had caused, because Grey enjoyed chaos and destruction. This gave White just the chance she needed. She came up from behind Grey and Black and caught them by surprise, using powers that neither Martin nor Dan understood to send Black and Grey so far away that they would not be a problem to anyone for a while.

Fillip came back to find White standing outside of the house with Dan and Martin. Following behind him were all of Martin's friends who had been captured by Jace. They were all exhausted but thrilled to be out. They knew that they were on their way home soon. Fillip ran to join his father and brother.

Home at Last

_30_

After Grey and Black had disappeared, everyone was eager to learn of the others' adventures. Arnold, one of Martin's colleagues, spoke,

"Shortly after you left the fourth dimension, the boy Jace came and was furious with us, saying that we weren't supposed to be there. At first we weren't very afraid of a boy his size. Why should we have been? Everything we did to try to deter him didn't work. We asked him: if we weren't allowed to be there, why was he? That made him even more furious. He left, we thought for good, but then he returned a little while later. That's when the trouble began.

"First Lemmy got it. He started rolling around on the ground screaming and no one had any idea what had happened until we noticed that the kid was chuckling, and grinning a horrible grin. He had controls that could cause excruciating pain. I thought it must take a lunatic to create something like that. Well, that boy proved himself to be a lunatic more than once if you ask me. After torturing all of us, we listened.

"At that point, Jones suggested that we would all like to leave now and go back to the third dimension, but I knew that wasn't going to work either. The boy told us that this was the final straw, and that we were not going to get any second chances now. He then used a consciousness inhibitor and we all blacked out. He took us to what he called "the house" and kept us there until now, when Fillip came down and got us out."

There was a long silence. It stretched on for minutes, but it felt like hours. They felt terrible that Jace had gotten away at the last moment. Then Fillip broke the silence and said, "He is a horrible person. I hate him!" Martin and Dan just looked at him without saying anything.

Then White created a warp and said, "This will take you back home to the third dimension." Without question, everyone went through the warp except Fillip. Fillip stayed behind to be with White a few minutes longer. Fillip knew she could tell what was going on inside of him. Hatred was all he ever thought about since he came upon Jace. He hated Jace and he promised himself that some day he would find him and he would lock him up.

He would never forget what Jace had done to him and the others. With that notion firmly stuck in his head, the knowledge that White knew exactly what he was thinking stayed with him as he walked through the warp and returned to the third dimension. "I will find you Jace," he thought, "and I will never forget."

Part Three:

Revenge

An Old Friend

31

After eight earth months, Mourndess was starting to get used to her new home. She still didn't know where that was and she hadn't heard it being called anything, so for the time being "here" was good enough for her. Finally she noticed that Pallk, the friendly alien who was making the pod, was coming outside more often, and if she looked very carefully at the right angle she could see some polished bulk above his house. He was done.

That night, she decided that she wouldn't stay here any longer. She snuck into Pallk's house that night. No one would ever suspect a wrong to be done here, so Pallk was fast asleep. She went out to the back of his house, his back yard. There sat a very well made pod. She got in. Mourndess looked at all the buttons and levers and after a while, figured out how it worked. So she turned it on and heard the engines roar. To her delight, by the time Pallk woke up she was so far away from the planet that there would be absolutely no hope of seeing her in the night sky.

It was the first wrong that ever happened there. When everyone woke up the next day, there was a lot of commotion. Nothing that terrible had ever happened to them. Their perfectly peaceful planet had just been ruined, and for a short period of time, the planet was corrupted. Then, a great white cloud passed over them and they were calm.

After that, Mourndess was forgotten completely, and no one knew that there had ever been a wrongdoing there. Its peace had returned and the planet went on the way it had been before Mourndess had arrived. Everyone was happy, and no one who was still on the planet would ever suspect that there had been someone named Mourndess there just a while ago, and that she had taken off with someone else's pod. No one would know, except for one.

A Warm Welcome

32

Mourndess noticed by looking at the angles of the stars and planets that if she went straight at the pod's top speed, she could track a course for home. So she waited. It's not like she wasn't used to waiting. Eventually, her home was in sight.

Within no time, Mourndess was sitting in a floating lounger in her kitchen in her home, her space station. But she was not going to stay there for very long. She needed to pack some gear onto her belt. She had not gone all that way just to go home and drink some tea. She came back for revenge; she was overwhelmed by her need for revenge.

She would get Mathonog and Soseph, she would get them back for what they did, and she would get the Shattering Device and do the task she, Mathonog, and Soseph each constantly wanted to complete. She would do it, not them! She promised herself she would, and she would destroy anything or anyone that got in her way.

Mathonog was furious. After being yelled at by Soseph for failing to kill Martin and being emotionally tortured by three humans and a bite-sized machine, Mathonog felt that he was going insane. But even insanity wasn't enough to overcome his intelligence. He would wait. Taking Martin now, right after everything that had happened, would not be very smart. Martin would be too prepared.

So Mathonog waited, and watched. There were satellite cameras in most of the rooms in Martin's house, even in his office at his work. Martin didn't know about these of course, but even so, Martin was always prepared. Jess followed Martin everywhere and the two boys stayed together, carrying transporters to either teleport them to Jess or their house. They always carried weapons that could freeze or paralyze others, which they never misused.

Mathonog could barely stand it, but he managed to overcome his boredom for a little bit longer. Martin, Dan, and Fillip had returned to their normal lives. Fillip went to school, Martin to his inventions, and

Dan returned to his studies. But Mathonog waited and waited and, finally, he saw his chance.

Just as Mathonog had done, Fillip waited until the others would not expect it. This was the first day in all of that time that Martin had not made them promise to be careful. He had finally gotten to a point where he trusted that they weren't in immediate danger. He felt relaxed, although he was still cautious enough to take Jess to work with him, along with all the weapons. When Fillip came home from school, his father was still at work and his brother had just left with a group of friends to go study. Dan had left a transmission to Fillip on the kitchen counter saying, "Be careful. I will be out with my friends studying until 6:00. Use your communicator if you need to reach me."

It surprised Fillip that his brother was still worried. It had, after all, been eight months since anything irregular had happened to them. I will be careful, he thought, and then he went into his father's study and packed things that might come in handy. As he had promised himself, he hadn't forgotten Jace. They had never told anybody about the fifth dimension. "When I get home, I'll have to tell dad that maybe we should," Fillip thought. Fillip then went into his father's room. By now he knew by heart exactly how to unlock the Connector and create a warp to the fourth dimension. He did that now, using a set of keys that Martin had given him in case of emergency. After looking back at the house and pausing for a few seconds, he then straightened up and walked thought the warp, thinking, I haven't forgotten, Jace. I'll find you.

Mathonog immediately set a warp for right where Fillip was to appear in the fourth dimension, and was about to activate the sequence when a transmission appeared right in front of his eyes. It was Soseph. He looked frantic, and said,

"Mathonog, come now! There is a ship on my scanner. When I look from the computer view I can visibly see her! She's back!" Soseph didn't say who "she" was, but Mathonog had no doubt who it was either. The transmission changed to Soseph's computer view and Mathonog saw the ship, with the driver - Mourndess Zlenwood! He looked back at the warp he had just made and then stared at the transmission. He ran as fast as he could to the nearest transport pod.

Fillip found himself in the fourth dimension, just as planned. He was actually in the exact same site he was in when he had first gone through that warp over a year ago, with billions of tents set up. He wondered once more how the tents had gotten there, just waiting for them to arrive in the fourth dimension, as if someone had been expecting them...He snapped out of his trance and remembered that he had other business to attend to. He really didn't have a good idea where Jace's house was from here so he decided to wander, determined to find somewhere that he recognized from his last expedition in the fourth dimension.

Mathonog arrived at Soseph's station just in time, before Mourndess did. They looked at each other, both seeing the terror on the other one's face. How had she returned? It was impossible! Before they got to say anything, the bell rang. "I'll get that," Soseph said slowly. With trembling hands, Soseph slowly walked to the portal and opened it. Mathonog and Soseph were both prepared with their stun guns. They did not think this would be pretty.

As soon as Soseph opened the portal, gun in hand, a mechanical octopus flew in, grabbed him by the neck, and lifted him in the air. The octopus had four, sharp tentacles and had the equivalent of jet packs all around its body, allowing it to fly very fast and very hard. It then flew to the wall, put him back down again, and drove its four tentacles into the wall, two on either side of his neck, holding Soseph fast. Before Mathonog could do anything, another octopus caught him around his waist. They were both trapped there and they realized that these creatures were much stronger than they were. They couldn't budge no matter how hard they pushed.

They were immobilized, and across the room, Mourndess entered the doorway and looked at them with mocking fake sympathy plastered on her face. She grinned and said, "Hello, boys." When she entered, around 10 more of the four-legged octopi flew in after her.

The Beginning of Her Revenge

33

Fillip kept on going, sprinting until he found a spot he recognized. It was difficult, considering that the last time he went through that forest he was running, and he had gone only a short distance before he had run through a warp. But he was sure that it was the same place he had seen last time, and he knew that the house was to the right. So that's where he went. He slowed down to a walk, so that he wouldn't be panting when he entered the house.

When Fillip got there, he entered through the front portal and there right in front of him was Jace.

As soon as Fillip entered the house he was flung against the wall. But Fillip was fast enough to turn around immediately and kick just in time to knock Jace back. Fillip got up. Jace was lying on the floor and he said, "I've been expecting you." Fillip jumped at him, but he rolled over and kicked him in the side, hard enough to make him curl up into a ball. Jace got up. "Don't make me laugh," he said. "What gives you the slightest idea that you can beat me, in any way at all? I want to-" He was interrupted by a kick in the side.

"Because I've done it before," Fillip boldly said. The fighting went on.

Mourndess started walking back and forth and finally she said, "Come." The two octopi released their prisoners, who fell to the floor wheezing. Soseph was coughing as well. Mourndess stepped on Soseph and leaned right up to his ear and said, "Remember me?"

He remembered her. She laughed and walked straight over Mathonog. She had taken all their weapons off of them, so they were now unarmed. When she walked away, both Mathonog and Soseph ran at her, but she was expecting them. She stepped to the side and both of them collided with each other in mid-air. She then said calmly, "Get them."

The twelve octopi flew at Mathonog and Soseph. Soseph quickly pulled out two metal containers and pried them open, just like he had done the last time he was with Mourndess. Out of the containers came two beams of light that coalesced into two leathery humanoid forms. They both turned solid.

"Protect us!" Soseph shouted. They did just that; they crossed their arms and stood in front of Soseph and Mathonog. The octopi tried to get past them but each time they did, one of the humanoid creatures grabbed at them or punched them. The octopi were very powerful for such small robotics, but not powerful enough to overcome the leathery creatures. While this was going on, Mathonog and Soseph tried very hard to catch their breath and Mourndess stood there, watching the commotion.

"How did you...do it? How did you escape?" Mathonog asked Mourndess.

"I didn't," Mourndess replied, "I was freed."

"How did you get freed? Who freed you??" Soseph asked in amazement.

"I can't tell you how...It's a secret," Mourndess said with a smile. Soseph got up and Mathonog followed without question.

"Bring them forward," he said to the leathery creatures. They grunted and slowly started walking forward, beating on the octopi whenever they clung on to their leathery skin. The creatures stopped occasionally to catch an octopus that had started to sneak away. Mathonog and Soseph started creeping to the side, away from the fight.

Unfortunately, Mourndess was prepared for this and held out a spray canister that was also used on their last encounter. These leathery creatures were in some way related to cats, and the canister was filled with a liquid extract of pure catnip leaves. She had already killed both of these creatures on their last encounter, but that didn't seem to matter to them, as they were probably either recreated or had never actually died in the first place. She sprayed three times, which did the trick. As before, they fell on the ground and started purring, consumed by the smell of the catnip. The robotic octopi found that now they could go straight past the creatures without any trouble. Their main target, Mathonog and Soseph, were only a few feet away from them.

The octopi flew straight in, but now it was Mathonog's turn to act. In one quick motion he activated a shielding screen, and Mathonog and Soseph were surrounded in a bubble of protection. It wasn't permanent and would eventually pop, but it gave them enough time to think of what they were going to do next. The bubble provided one-way protection, so that whoever was on the inside could see and get out while those on the outside could not see or get in. It was a very ingenious form of unilateral protection that was created by Mathonog himself. Currently, however, this handy bubble protection was not being put to use at all, considering they still had no idea what they were going to do as soon as the bubble popped.

Finally, Mathonog had an idea. He told Soseph his plan, and after he got Soseph's approval, he set it into action. They first scooted the bubble to the right near a cabinet. As quickly as Mathonog could he stuck his hand out, pulled open one of the drawers, and pulled three objects from the drawer and pulled them back into the protection of the bubble.

This was his plan. The robotic octopi were made of iron. He could tell this because they were magnetically attracted to the chest, which had a quite powerful magnet in it. Iron rusted. Mathonog could make them rust the same way he could make any piece of iron rust, by turning it into iron oxide. He located the octopi in the screen of his rust stimulator and activated the machine. Mathonog's machine could create a vacuum next to each of the octopi, following them and constantly filling them with air. In a few years, rust would form and slow them down.

But they didn't have a few years. Mathonog then use his aging activator, which could successfully speed up the aging process of many substances, including iron. For centuries there had been a search for a mechanism to slow down the aging process, but that had been unsuccessful. Mathonog kept the age activator going long enough for rust to become heavy on all the robots and to slow them down significantly. Shortly they were severely immobilized; they couldn't fly any more because the metal air pump had become rusted. Then Mathonog took a blast gun that could knock the creatures back. With one carefully aimed shot, he knocked all of the robotic octopi across the room where they slammed into the wall. The robots got up and slowly made their way across the room. Meanwhile, Mourndess was running out of catnip.

Fillip's Fight

34

Fillip finally rolled away from Jace and got up. He was panting laboriously. His breath eventually slowed, while he watched Jace get up. His lip was swollen and bleeding.

"I've been expecting you," Jace said.

"I know," Fillip said. "You will not be forgiven. No matter what it takes, I promise that I will always search for some way put you behind bars…in the third dimension." There was a short pause and then Jace said, "I know." Then he jumped at Fillip and they started fighting all over again.

A few minutes later, Fillip rolled away and got up, then backed away from Jace. He could not believe what he was doing. He was bleeding, bruised, and scratched almost everywhere! And he was eight years old! But his rage overcame his common sense and he couldn't stop fighting. Both boys did nothing for a few seconds, and then suddenly Jace's lips parted into a smile, which turned into a grin.

"Give up," he said, his neck now covered in veins.

"No!" Fillip shouted. Fillip ran at Jace as hard as he could, but before he could reach him he felt something hit him in the abdomen, hard. He realized that this was Jace's fist, but only after he was airborne. Fillip went flying about ten feet, straight through the open doorway, and landed on some dirt outside on his back. He stared in amazement at Jace. No one could have possibly hit him that hard.

Now that Fillip thought about it, how was it that he had survived that blow in the first place? Just as he thought this, he saw White only a few feet away. He dusted himself off. He noticed that he wasn't bleeding anymore; as a matter of fact, he wasn't even bruised. He at first thought it was magic, but then he remembered something his father had once told him. Anything can seem to be magical if you don't think it's possible. You could think that warps were magical, but if you lived in the fourth dimension you probably wouldn't. Fillip noticed that Jace was still advancing on him. When Fillip looked again he found that Grey and Black were following Jace, and Jace looked even madder than ever.

The International
Scientific Academy

35

Martin was excited. He had decided to finally go to the International Scientific Academy to tell them of his discovery of the fifth dimension. He wanted let them know about his discovery and also to warn them of its danger. The International Scientific Academy wasn't very difficult to find. It was quite possibly the largest building in the world. So he went there, and talked to the person at the entry station.

"What would you like?" the woman asked.

"I need to talk to the president," Martin said. She laughed.

"So does everybody else, but they don't get to. What is your story?"

"I am Martin Westle Parnes, and I have jut discovered the next dimension," Martin said calmly. She stared at him without saying anything, then said,

"...Top...Floor...I'll let him know you are coming." He walked over to the transporter. It felt a bit nauseating going up so fast, but the next second he was there. There was only one massive room at the top, with circular windows that provided a spectacular view of the skyline. There was one desk at the far end of the room and behind it was the president of the International Scientific Academy.

Martin had learned a few weeks after he had returned from the fifth dimension that the previous president, who had been involved in the decision about whether everyone should move to the fourth dimension or not the year before, had retired. Martin walked all the way across the room and stopped right in front of the desk. The new president leaned close to him and said,

"Are you...Martin Westle Parnes?" Martin nodded. The man chuckled and then said, "My name is Albert Rolnoldson. I've heard all about you. What now, have you discovered the fifth dimension?" He chuckled again. He stopped immediately when Martin nodded.

"No, really?" the president asked. Martin nodded again. The president got out of his chair and carried another chair to where Martin was. "Sit down," he said to Martin. "Tell me everything, from how and why you got there, to how and why you left."

Martin told him the whole story. He talked about how he found the warp by accident, how they met Jace, everything. The President sat there silently, listening to his whole story without a comment, and when Martin was finished, he didn't say anything. There was a pause, a very long pause, and then the president started laughing. "A nine-year-old? Doing all that?" Martin felt a little defensive and said, "It's true!" But the president didn't seem to be listening. He was thinking about how the discovery of the fifth dimension could possibly give him a piece of fame and fortune.

"Take me there," The president suddenly said.

"I can't. It's dangerous! Weren't you listening? You could get killed!" Martin protested. The president leaned right up close to him and said,

"You can do what you are told, Martin Westle Parnes, and I have told you to take me to the fifth dimension." The president was, of course, a very important man in the scientific community. He had no choice. Martin sighed.

"All right," Martin said, "When do you want to leave?"

"Now."

"We are going to have to go to my house-" Martin was interrupted when the president pointed to a booth in the corner of the room that Martin hadn't noticed before. Then the president said, "Use the teleporter." Martin nodded and they both went into the booth. Martin typed in the code for his house and then they were there. Martin got out of the booth. Fillip and Dan would have been out of school at this time but Martin didn't see them anywhere. He walked to his room and saw that that the Connector was already out, and there was a warp right there. Normally, he would be very suspicious. But he wasn't given that kind of liberty right now. The president pointed to the warp and said,

"Is that it?"

"No," Martin answered. The president didn't say anymore. Martin set the warp the same way he had done the last time he had gone to the fifth dimension and pressed the button. Just like last time, there was a flash that covered the entire room and Martin and the president of the International Scientific Academy were teleported to the fifth dimension.

Yargentia was excited, very excited. Someone had actually gotten out! She knew that it had to be that woman, Rewortan, because she had wanted to leave the planet as well. She ran to Pallk, who was quite well known as being a good builder. She saw him a little ways off and quickened her pace, saying "excuse me" to everything she bumped into. She caught up with Pallk. Pallk looked at her and said, "Yes, what is it?"

Yargentia had been running and was out of breath. Once she had caught her breath, she said, "Pallk, would it be possible for you to build me a transport pod?" Pallk thought about that for a few seconds. Then he looked back at her and said,

"Yes, I believe I could do that, but it might take a while. I had plans to build myself one too."

"That would be wonderful! Thank you, very much!" Yargentia was very pleased indeed. Finally, she was going home! Back to her two boys, back to her husband! She could still see her boys so clearly in her mind, but the last time she had seen them her oldest had been 15 years old and her youngest was only 4. She was having a hard time visualizing Dan and Fillip four years older now.

Although she remembered the last incident with a pod she had had, she was still hopeful. Someone else had gotten out, so she was sure she would be able to as well. She ran around the little town, freely expressing her joy to everyone she met. It was truly possible that she was finally going home!

Their Escape

<u>36</u>

The robotic octopi continued their slow creaky crawl across the room. Luckily for Mathonog and Soseph it was a very large room, and they were still in their bubble. But there was more to Mathonog's plan. Mathonog reached out of the bubble again and opened up another drawer. He took out a warp that he was planning on using when they really needed it. For now, they just sat back and watched. Mourndess had run out of catnip before the octopi reached the bubble. The leathery creatures got up slowly and walked to the bubble.

"Protect us still," Soseph said. The creatures took the same defensive pose in front of the bubble. Then Mourndess laughed and took out a weapon she had been saving. At that point Mathonog and Soseph realized that Mourndess had too many tricks up her sleeve. Soseph opened up the metal containers, and the leathery creatures turned back into their light forms and vanished into the boxes. Then Mathonog used the warp to transport Soseph and himself to the fifth dimension.

Mourndess took out her own scanner to look for Mathonog and Soseph. She wasn't giving up.

Jace's Mistake

37

Fillip quickly scrambled back, but he knew it was no use. He could feel Grey staring at him and he knew he was the target. Grey was advancing on him and Jace was following right behind Grey. Grey said, "I can do this on my own."

But then Jace said, "I don't need you anymore! Look at me!" Jace laughed. Fillip then realized that both White and Black were trying to hold Grey back and seemed to be failing, and that Grey was much bigger than he usually was. Grey chuckled a bit and then finally said,

"Fine. I shall enjoy this." There was a small bang and Grey flew straight into White and Black. All three spirits hurtled off into the distance, bashing into each other occasionally as they flew off. Fillip quickly looked back at Jace and saw that Jace was looking on after White, Black, and Grey as well. What did it all mean? How did Jace know Grey? Is that how he got all his powers?   Fillip's thoughts were interrupted when Jace suddenly looked at Fillip and smiled.

"You'll never catch me," he said. Suddenly, a warp appeared right behind him. It looked different than all the others Fillip had seen. This one was red and blue. Jace walked backwards into the warp and disapeared, to wherever that warp went. The warp was still there, and the Fillip felt a sick feeling rising n his throat. He knew that this warp would take him to another dimension. He stepped through the warp.

Getting In Mourndess' Way

38

Martin blinked when the warp disappeared and he was once more in the fifth dimension, but this time with quite different company than last time. Martin watched the president of the International Scientific Academy stare at everything around him. He observed the trees, the ground, the sky, the rocks, the water, everything. Then he recorded it all in into a transcorder, and continued measuring something else.

Martin sat down and watched this silently, and when the man finally put away his tools and sat down with a very surprised and happy look on his face, Martin said,

"Albert, aren't people at your work going to notice that you are missing? You are the President of the Academy."

"No, I go missing all the time. There are many projects that will in some way take me away or require me to leave. They won't mind." Martin didn't say anything in response to that; he just sat there until Albert said, "Get up. We are going to look around."

"Fine," Martin said as he got up and stretched. Before he knew it, Albert was quite far away, still examining more plants and rocks with fascination. Martin ran and easily caught up with Albert, but when he did, he was panting.

"Can we slow down a little bit?" Martin asked in between breaths.

"Okay," Albert said, "More time to examine things." So they kept on walking and Albert kept on thoroughly measuring and examining things and then recording it in his notebook the entire day. Everything was different here in the fifth dimension, and Albert was searching for anything that could be used for new inventions.

When Mourndess' scanner showed where Mathonog and Soseph were, Mourndess already had her warping device out and ready to be used. Within seconds she was a few feet away from them. Mathonog and Soseph were on their minipod and were speeding away. In no time Mourndess was also on her minipod, right on their heels.

Mathonog and Soseph were both very experienced drivers when it came to the minipods. So was Mourndess. But Mathonog and Soseph had an advantage over Mourndess. They knew where they were going. Still, Mourndess was gaining on them. Whether it was because she had less weight on her pod or she was a more experienced driver or she was just lucky, she slowly started to gain on them.

At about that same time Martin and Albert were taking a break. Albert was describing a dream he had the night before. Martin tried to explain to him about MindLite and Albert listened with fascination, again searching for possibilities of harnessing the idea commercially. Martin lay down to rest as Albert continued to look around the fifth dimension. Martin hadn't managed to get any sleep the night before because Albert had him look out in case any animals or strange creatures came by. Martin knew that there wouldn't be any, but he did what he was told.

Martin was finally asleep when Albert turned around and shook him awake. When Martin was fully awake Albert said, "Do you still believe that there is a nine-year-old boy here in the fifth dimension?" When Martin nodded Albert said, "Show me." Martin stared at him in disbelief. Albert turned around so he was facing away from Martin and didn't say anything more for a while. Then suddenly, before Martin was given a chance to react, Albert turned around and in a flash put a loose metallic substance around Martin's neck.

Before Martin got a chance to move, Albert used his controls to tighten the collar around Martin's neck. It wasn't tight enough to strangle him or cut off his air supply, but tight enough so that Martin could not get it off.

"Get up," Albert commanded. Then he said, "Take me to this boy, Jace." Martin immediately got up. He knew what this was. It was a metallic collar with many holes in it, and it had a needle that was attached to it with a substance called gluemax. Gluemax was the strongest and fastest adhesive discovered to date, that would disappear when put under a weak electric pulse and was made to be resistant to most frictional forces.

The needle on the collar was made entirely of titanium except for the back, which was iron. If Albert pressed the button, it would send an electric pulse to the collar that turned it into an electromagnet. This magnet would then pull the needle through the collar and into Martin's neck. This was, of course, highly illegal, and Martin couldn't believe that Albert, the president of the International Scientific Academy was using it to get what he wanted. But, then again, Albert was probably used to getting anything he wanted. And something now seemed very important to him.

Martin was shocked and angry, but mostly scared. That didn't mean he didn't have a plan, of course. He triggered the mechanism to a device he had with him, attached to his hand. If he ever managed to get out of the fifth dimension and back to he third alive, then Albert would get what he deserved.

Mourndess had finally gotten as close to Mathonog and Soseph as she had been last time. She was again interrupted before she managed to press the button, but this time Mathonog and Soseph hadn't made any sudden turns. As a matter of fact, before she fully understood what had happened, she was hurtled out the front window of her pod, which was open, and crashed into a tree. Before it happened, she saw two men walking, one of them she recognized from watching Mathonog and Soseph searching for him: Martin Westle Parnes. Apparently Mathonog and Soseph had seen him too.

Soseph crashed into Mathonog; Soseph stopped while Mathonog kept on going and hit the tree. Right after they had crashed into each other, they dropped out of the emergency exits on the bottom of the pods, with a pocket-pack on their backs and their trusty light-beings at their sides. They were lucky, because right after they dropped out their pods erupted in flames.

The lower half of Mourndess' pod rammed into a tree and Mourndess went flying onto the ground near Mathonog and Soseph. Her pod was broken and would be nonfunctional until she could get it repaired. Martin and Albert were just standing there, watching the commotion. Then, Albert asked Martin, "I thought you said that no one lived here except that kid."

Martin said, "They don't live here. I don't know what they are doing here. I know who they are..." He slowly turned his head towards all three of them and then finally pointed to Mourndess last. Then he said, "Except for that one. But I could guess that those men," he pointed to Mathonog and Soseph, "would be here for me. But, from the looks of things, it seems that she" he pointed to Mourndess "was chasing them," he pointed to Mathonog and Soseph again. "At least that's what I think happened."

Mourndess pushed herself up and looked around. She just stood there for a few seconds, and then did the only thing that seemed reasonable to her at the time. She turned around, ran to the tree that her pod crashed into, jumped up and grabbed a branch. She threw herself over it, and slowly started making her way up the tree towards where her pod crashed. For the time being Mathonog and Soseph were still lying on the ground, apparently unconscious from their fall.

Martin turned towards Albert and said, "We have to get out of here before those two men lying on the ground get up. Because when that happens, I suspect we both will die!" Martin thought that he was making his point clear enough, but apparently it wasn't clear enough for Albert.

Albert pointed to the controls for the collar, "No, I want a closer look. I want to figure out what is going on, and I think this is going to be fun." He grinned. Martin didn't know how Albert defined the word 'fun' and he didn't particularly want to know either.

Dan arrived home soon after his father had left with Albert. But, because time passed quite differently in the different dimensions, the day and a half that Martin and Albert had spent in the fifth dimension took a few minutes in the third. Dan noticed immediately that neither his brother nor his father was home and then thought about their last visit to the fifth dimension. Dan slammed the door and ran to Martin's room. The Connector was out, and the locks had been broken. Dan grabbed the device and set it to the fifth dimension, but before he pressed the button, he called out for Jess, who came flying into the room.

"What is it?" she asked him.

"They're gone," Dan said, bringing his attention back to the Connector.

Jess gasped, and then, after a pause, said calmly, "Well there's no time to lose then!"

Dan nodded and made the warp appear that would take them to the fifth dimension, to save Martin.

The Dimensions Beyond

39

Fillip opened his eyes. He tried again to make sense of it all, but it was no use. Whether his eyes were open or not he still saw complete darkness. He tried moving around. The only thing that assured him that he had moved at all was the knowledge that he had attempted to move. He couldn't feel anything, not even the ground or his clothes moving when he moved. He couldn't hear anything except his own breathing, but the fact that he even heard that was very reassuring to him. Then he heard a noise, a high-pitched noise. He realized that it must be Jace. He listened more carefully and then he heard Jace's voice say,

"Noooooooo! The dimension of death! Must get to my warp. Must find it without feeling it. Where is it? Come on, my time is running out!" Jace kept on talking, but Fillip stopped listening. He had an idea. Fillip started walking until he heard Jace's voice getting louder. Moving was quite difficult when he couldn't feel the ground, but. Fillip started running, following the voice. Jace's voice was saying, "Come on, come on! Oh why did I come here, why? The seventh dimension..."

Then the voice stopped. Fillip kept on running, and then apparently ran straight into another warp. He blinked. The 8th dimension. At least he could see now. But that was it, he could only see, which was an odd feeling. He could not feel anything, smell, hear, or taste. He could just see. All he had to do was look at a place and see that he was there, and he would be there. But he must truly see himself going there, instead of actually going there. He barely understood it himself, but here, it made perfect sense.

Then Fillip saw Jace, who was moving away quickly. So Fillip saw himself following Jace even faster. He managed to keep pace with Jace although he felt himself getting very tired. Eventually he got a break when Jace slowed down. Fillip stopped and rested because he knew what was going to happen next. Jace was seeing himself take out the warp, set the coordinates and send them into the next dimension.

Fillip was too tired to stop Jace, and felt he would need more energy for whatever dimension was next. He guessed it would be the 9th dimension next. He really couldn't tell for sure, but liked giving them a number for some type of reference. Eventually Jace managed to envision getting his warp device out and creating another warp. This one, like the warp to the fifth dimension, spread out and took both Fillip and Jace without them needing to go to through it. Then they were in what Fillip would call the 9th dimension. That meant that he was four dimensions away from his family. And he wasn't stopping there.

Dan and Jess appeared in the fifth dimension. They saw smoke in the distance and figured out that there was a good chance that Martin and Albert were there. So that was where Jess and Dan headed. It was quite far away, so Dan ran and Jess just flew to keep up with him. Now would not be a good time to get lost.

This time Fillip appeared in this new dimension and he could see nothing. This wasn't like the dimension of death, because he didn't actually see black. He saw nothing, no colors at all, and that meant not even black. It was a strange feeling, one that he would not be able to describe well to anyone who wasn't actually there to feel it. Fillip could not hear anything, or smell anything either. Or feel anything for that matter, but he could taste everything. He knew which direction to go in because it was his judgment, his taste.

It was different here in this dimension, better. Fillip could taste things like fear or movement, and even be able to tell what someone was doing. Fillip could taste the inside of his mouth, and wanted to taste everything outside his mouth too, but knew that it would not be a very smart idea. He trusted his judgment and turned to the left. He started running, although it was a little slow going because he couldn't feel anything.

Fillip had to trust his judgment about what happened next. His judgment told him that he had been chasing Jace and that Jace had just turned around and hit him in the face. Fillip put his hand over the spot on his face where he though he got hit, even though he couldn't feel it. Then Fillip grabbed for something that he had brought along. If he used it, it would freeze Jace in place, allowing Fillip to use something else that he had brought - his father's Catcher. Then he could fit

Jace in its small bulk and Jace would be locked in there until Fillip let him out.

Fillip was about to use the freezing device when he was sucked into another warp, off to the next dimension. When Fillip entered this new dimension, he had a feeling it was another one of his five senses, but he couldn't tell which one yet. He couldn't taste the inside of his mouth, he couldn't see anything, he couldn't hear anything, even when he tried talking to himself, and he couldn't smell anything. That meant it had to be the dimension of feeling. Fillip put his hands out and felt a wall. It was made of brick. He felt his way along the wall, and tried moving as fast as he could.

Fillip then noticed that he felt Jace right in front of him, but before he could get his freezing device out they were both off to the next dimension. In this dimension he immediatly noticed that he smelled his own flesh. It felt quite weird; he could smell so many things at once and somehow identified one of them as Jace. From then on he just followed his scent, but as with the last few dimension, before he managed to freeze Jace, they were off again.

This time, Fillip knew what the dimension he was in had to be. He had already done feel, smell, see, and taste so this had to be the dimension of hearing. Fortunately, the only thing he could hear was footsteps and he was sure they were Jace's. Unfortunately, he could hear very well, so this heightened hearing took a bit of getting used to before he could tell how far away Jace was. But as soon as he had caught up with Jace, like all of the times before, they were off to the next dimension. They had already gone through all of the senses that Fillip knew of, so he had no idea what would happen in the next dimension. He believed he was heading into the 13th dimension.

The Great Shattering Device

40

Mourndess had finished climbing up the tree and was back in her minipod. She packed everything she would need and pressed a button on the control panel of the pod. This button would take the pod back to her station where it would immediately start repairing itself. She, of course, had planned to go with it but she was thrown back out of the pod and it took off without her. She may have wondered why she had gone flying out of her pod but her mind was more preoccupied with other things. For example, at that moment she noticed that she was flying head first towards the ground, fast enough to easily break her neck on the ground below.

Just in time, she managed to trigger the release of several claw-shaped creatures. "Save me!" Before she hit the ground the creatures used their bodies to form a floating air-raft and completely stopped her fall. She then said, "Take me down." They did as they were told and took her down to the ground.

Mourndess saw that the reason she had gone flying out of her pod was because two of Soseph's light-beings had been shaking the tree. It was only then that she noticed that Mathonog and Soseph had gotten up and were standing quite near her. She also noticed that the man she had not recognized previously was standing up and watching her closely, while moving slowly towards the three of them, and that Martin was following behind the man very slowly.

"I'm Mourndess," she said to Martin, but the stranger in front of him thought that she was talking to him.

"I'm Albert, and this is…"

"Martin. Yes, I know." Mourndess finished his sentence for him, and then continued, "If you were sent to bring him here, then you can go now. He is the only one needed, the only one they need." She gestured towards Mathonog and Soseph. "Martin is the only one who is important here."

Albert seemed to take that personally, and argued, "Actually, back in the third dimension, I am much more important than he is. I am the president of one of the largest institutions on Earth, and I want some of my questions answered."

Mourndess appeared to be whispering something. As soon as Albert finished speaking, one of Mourndess' claw creatures flew for his neck and pinned him against a tree. It was loose enough for him to speak, but he said nothing, just looked around wildly. It occurred to Albert at this point that maybe he was in over his head. Martin took a small step forward, towards Mourndess, Mathonog, and Soseph. He looked at Mourndess and said, "I don't know you. How is it that you know me?" Mourndess looked at him for a few seconds, and then said,

"You probably already know that Mathonog and Soseph are after you."

"I also know that it has something to do with a device, or at least I believe that is what it is," Martin said.

"Yes, the Shattering Device. You've probably figured out that I know these two." She pointed at Mathonog and Soseph, and Martin nodded slowly. Then she continued, "We have known each other all of our lives, and for many years now we've known each other as rivals, over the Shattering Device. We all want to get the Shattering Device and unlock its secret, its purpose, but they want it for their own use and I want it for mine. There is only one main use of the Shattering Device, and it can only be used once. Then it will be forever destroyed. You yourself could not use it, because you came from here."

Martin was confused and said, "No, I came from the third dimension."

"I know, but there is more out there than just dimensions." There was a pause. Then something in Mourndess' pocket beeped, and she took it out. She stared at the screen for a few seconds, and then put it back in her pocket. She looked up at Martin and continued, "It seems that your son, Fillip and someone named Jace have just skipped the sixth dimension, and jumped, dimension by dimension, from the seventh to the thirteenth dimension. Mathonog, Soseph and I are all from the sixth dimension."

Martin frantically looked around, but he knew that he could probably not do anything about it at the moment. He had no way of getting to the 13th dimension himself, and he had a feeling that no one was about to take him there. So the best he could do was stay here, and hope for the best.

Mourndess continued, "But you can say that the Shattering Device is quite picky. You can't just press a button and it's done, there are quite a few things that must happen first. In the case of Mathonog and Soseph, they have to kill you before they can fully use the Shattering Device. I am a rival of Mathonog and Soseph, and don't want to give them the chance to use the Shattering Device, which means that I must protect you at all costs."

"But don't you have to kill me too?" Martin asked. He wasn't sure that this was a smart thing to say at the moment.

"No, it's different for different people." Mourndess knew that she really didn't have to protect Martin because the Shattering Device would continue to select a different person at random, unless you were to enter the secret code, which only Mourndess knew. Mathonog and Soseph did not know that, of course, and it would best to keep them off course for as long as possible.

Martin interrupted her thoughts. "Whom do you have to kill?" he asked her.

"It would not be wise of me to tell you that, because then Mathonog and Soseph would try to prevent that from happening." She looked over at Mathonog and Soseph, who were just standing there watching. "Anyway, be happy that you're safe, because I will work to protect you at all costs. So, are we friends?" She put out her hand to shake.

After a few seconds Martin shook his head. He said, "I am enemies with Mathonog and Soseph, so whatever they're after, whatever this Shattering Device does, I want to prevent it from happening. But I know that you want this Shattering Device just as much as they do. I don't understand what this great device can accomplish, but I am worried that it will not be good. Whether you're trying to protect me or not, that makes us enemies." Mourndess put her hand down. She whispered something and the claw device released Albert.

Albert understood this turn of events, and spoke up, this time to Mathonog. "So you want Martin dead. Is that it?" Martin realized to his immediate horror that he still had that metal collar on and that he could be killed any second. And that would mean that Mathonog and Soseph could get what they wanted after all. After Mathonog nodded, Albert continued, "Do you recognize the collar Martin is wearing?" Mathonog nodded again. Albert pulled out the control and said, "What's your price?"

Mathonog smiled and then said, "Money really isn't any problem for me. I can get you whatever amount you want, in whatever currency you use."

Albert looked convinced and said, "It's a deal; I'll let you do the honors." Albert was about to hand Mathonog the device.

Mourndess then said, "I can't let you do this!" She called to her claw creatures just as Soseph's light-beings were also called into action. "Defend me!" she cried. The claw devices did as they were told and kept the light-creature just out of range of grabbing Mourndess. Just then, as Mourndess was telling her claw devices to take the controls from Albert, there was a large bolt of electrical charge from behind her, and she fell down to the ground, unconscious. Standing behind her was Mathonog with a stun gun that was not strong enough to kill her, but strong enough to keep her out for a few hours at least.

Mathonog grinned and said to Albert, "Where were we?" Mathonog laughed and walked toward Albert. Martin watched in horror as his death moved closer, one step at a time.

Part Four:

A Second Chance

The Thirteenth Dimension
with Jace

_41_

Fillip looked around in this dimension and was glad to find that he could see normally. As a matter of fact, he could also taste, hear, smell, and feel normally too. He was on grass, and he could see trees, rocks, and mountains in the distance. Everything was the same color as it was in the third dimension. He really didn't have that much proof that he wasn't actually back in the third dimension, after all, except for the fact that he couldn't see people or buildings or any other sign of humans. Fillip knew that in the third dimension, at least on Earth, he was rarely alone.

Fillip began to get scared. He was alone. Suddenly, it began to rain, thunder booming in the distance. Then Fillip realized that maybe this dimension had something to do with his emotions, and that he could be causing the thunder storm. Fillip immediately calmed himself. The rain and thunder stopped and the clouds moved just enough so that there was a sliver of sunlight touching Fillip. He smiled. He felt his confidence rising, even more than it had when he was stuck in Jace's jail. He knew that he was going to catch Jace once and for all. This was it. The sun burned the clouds away completely.

In the distance, Fillip saw Jace running frantically. There was no light shining on him, although no clouds were in the sky and the sun was shining fiercely. Nonetheless, Jace had stopped and fallen to his knees. Fillip caught up with him in no time. Just before Fillip froze Jace with his deaminator, Fillip caught a glimpse of Jace's face. Fillip knew that something was different. Jace looked like an ordinary boy his age, not grinning or mad; his eyes weren't bloodshot any more and there were no visible veins popping out of his skin.

Fillip wondered what could have happened, recalling the time in the jail when Jace had looked like this, and had given him the keys. Fillip pitied Jace, although he didn't understand what this change meant. He feared that this change could still be part of a trap, and he knew what his task was at the moment. Fillip froze Jace and took Jace's warp creator. After studying the warp creator, Fillip understood how to make a warp to the third dimension. Before Fillip left, he used the Catcher and stored Jace safely inside. Soon he found himself right outside his house, in the third dimension.

Fillip was greeted by his dog who whined, barked and wagged his tail furiously. He wouldn't let Fillip out of his sight. Fillip quickly realized that Martin and Dan were not there. He had a feeling that they were in the fifth dimension and he knew that he should go and find them, but he was exhausted and had jumped through enough dimensions for one day. He decided that he would wait for them to return, and do something about Jace when they arrived. He put his pack down and carefully put the Catcher in a position so that it could not roll over and automatically release Jace.

Fillip went into his father's room where he found the Connector. He remembered how, as soon as they had returned from the fifth dimension, his father had activated a second part of the Connector so that he could make a warp from the fifth dimension and get back. Fillip decided that it would be the best place to wait for them. He sat down on a very comfortable lounger and immediately fell asleep, the dog nuzzling his head.

The Third Dimension Again

_42_

Dan and Jess were almost there. They put on one final burst of speed and made it out to the clearing just in time. Albert and Mathonog were standing side by side. Albert was giving Mathonog the controller for the collar and Mathonog was giving Albert some money. Dan and Jess were certain this was not a good development. Dan whispered something to Jess and she nodded. Dan ran out to the clearing.

"Hey!" he shouted at Mathonog and Albert. They turned to look at him. At that moment, Albert screamed and fell forward, clutching a small burn right at the back of his neck. The burn was quite small, and it looked like Albert had screamed more in surprise than pain. However, the controller flew in the air and Dan caught it. He ran to his father.

"What is this thing?" Dan asked Martin as soon as he caught up with him.

"I'll explain later. Just let me use it for a second." Dan handed it to Martin, who manipulated it and pulled off the collar. Dan noticed a small apparatus in Martin's hands with a light blinking in the front. He recognized the device immediately. It was a very small holo-video camera had had been attached and camouflaged in Martin's hand. That meant that Martin had recorded everything; everything Albert had just done to Martin was on tape.

Jess had been hard at work, and the area around Mathonog and Soseph was getting hotter and hotter. Mathonog and Soseph were creating a warp to leave, since they knew exactly what Jess was capable of doing. Mathonog and Soseph went through the warp in a split second and it disappeared behind them. Martin captured Albert inside the Catcher and created a warp which took them all back to the third dimension. All except Mourndess, who was lying unconscious on the ground.

When Mourndess finally woke up, she noticed immediately that she was alone, but was glad to find that her various tools were still there. She couldn't take it any longer; she would get the Shattering Device, she assured herself. And for one of the few times in her life, Mathonog and Soseph weren't going to get in her way; she would make sure of it.

Fillip was woken when a warp flashed and Martin, Dad, and Jess were standing in the room with him.

"Nice to see you're back," Fillip said to them.

"Nice to see you're still alive," Martin replied nonchalantly, then rushed over and gave his son a bear hug. He was so happy to see everyone back safely. "How was the thirteenth dimension?" Martin asked.

"Fine. How was the fifth?" Fillip said casually. Martin and Dan sat down on loungers, Jess sat on Fillip's head. The dog sat at Martin's feet.

"Maybe we should fill each other in on what happened," Fillip suggested after no one said anything for a while. "I'll go first," he said. He told them everything that happened from when he first left to go after Jace, to when Martin, Dad, and Jess returned from the fifth dimension.

Then Martin told his story from when he decided to tell the International Scientific Academy about the fifth dimension to when he returned to the third dimension with Dan and Jess, with Albert safely inside the Catcher. Then Dan told his story, with Jess's help, from when he found that Martin and Fillip were gone, to when he got back with Martin.

Martin then said, "You know, we should probably tell the authorities about Albert and Jace, so we can finally get them into custody, once and for all."

It was very easy for Martin to convince the authorities that they should put Jace into custody, even though he was only nine years old. They had the proof of his dangerous activities from Martin's co-workers and family, including Jess. It was much more difficult to convince them to imprison Albert, considering his high position. But once Martin showed them the holo-tape he had made, there was no doubt that he had broken enough laws to be arrested and tried.

Jace, however, was placed under the control and supervision of Martin, even though he was going to jail. Martin had to choose if Jace could have visitors and would decide when Jace could be released, if ever. Martin was given this duty because the court was unsure about imprisoning a nine-year-old, even if this nine-year-old had tried to kill anyone that entered a dimension other than the third, and had held five people hostage and tortured them, all for no reasonable cause.

After all this, to the surprise of Martin, Dan, Fillip, and Jess, Jace admitted that all of this had been true. And not with the kind of wicked pride that Fillip expected he would have, but with the kind of sadness and hopelessness he had displayed when Fillip had caught him. Fillip knew that there was something strange about Jace, and was determined to figure it out. He felt that Jace had been possessed, but was now free. Now Jace looked like an ordinary boy.

Many pieces of the puzzle had been put together, but Martin still could not rest. He had the feeling that something was stirring and he knew it had to do with Mathonog and Soseph. Martin had a portable transport pod that he kept in his own hangar, one that had been made three years before and was still quite new. Martin liked his pod and, of course, had a license to drive it, but he normally didn't use it much. Now, however, he had a use for it. He had decided that the mysterious Shattering Device must be something that could be used for evil purposes. At all costs he would stop Mathonog, Soseph, and Mourndess from getting the device. To do that, he would need this pod.

Martin entered the house to tell Fillip and Dan about how he was going to leave for a while. Martin opened his mouth to speak but before he started talking, Fillip himself started.

"Dad, something's weird about Jace and we all know it. I might be gone for a while every day, talking to Jace, figuring him out a little. Dan agreed to come with me because you know I'm not allowed to be there unless I'm with an adult…Okay?" Martin just stared at him for a few seconds. Then he finally said,

"Okay…I came to tell you that I might be gone for a while every day too, to make sure that Mathonog, Soseph, or Mourndess don't get the Shattering Device. I decided that I would make sure that they don't." Fillip stared at him for a few seconds, then said,

"Okay. I'll go tell Dan." Fillip left the room. Martin sighed. He went to his room to prepare for his journey.

Jace's Mystery

43

Fillip left the house with Dan later that day and headed for the jail where Jace was kept. Fillip was allowed to enter Jace's cell. Jace was sitting on the ground in his cell. Fillip was reminded of when he had been Jace's prisoner, which made him terribly sad. It was odd; he knew that he had done the right thing by putting Jace behind bars, and yet he felt wrong about doing it now. Jace looked up at him. Fillip spoke, with a note of frustration in his voice,

"Tell me; what's so different now. Why is it that all of a sudden I can trust you?" Jace said nothing, then looked down and sighed. Without looking back up he answered,

"Nothing. Nothing is different, you still can't..." he paused, and then rephrased his thought, "You shouldn't trust me. But something is different now. He's gone. Now my life means nothing." Fillip looked at him, confused.

"Who's gone?" But Jace would not answer; he just kept repeating, under his breath,

"He's gone. My life is over." Eventually Fillip left with Dan to go back home, but he continued to ponder what Jace had said.

Martin was ready to go. He used his Catcher to make the travel pod small enough to fit in his pocket, and then created a warp to the fourth dimension. He knew Mathonog and Soseph now lived in the fourth dimension, and guessed it was also where Mourndess lived too. Once in the fourth dimension, Martin brought his pod to full size and got in. He thought that maybe he should have brought Jess along. As if in answer to this thought, Jess popped through the warp and told Martin that she wanted to go with him. They got in the pod and took off.

Fillip was thinking about what Jace had said but it just didn't make any sense to him. "He's gone." Who could Jace have meant? Fillip thought about that for the rest of the day, and also as he was going to sleep. "Perhaps a good night's sleep will help me think," he thought.

When Fillip woke up, he found that he had been right the night before. He remembered what Jace had said to Grey. Maybe Grey was the one Jace was referring to. Fillip thought about that for a while. Later, another thought came to mind, maybe, just maybe, Grey had something to do with Jace being so angry and violent, and now that he was gone, Jace was calmer. It may have also been the reason why, when Grey, Black, and White were outside of Jace's prison fighting, Jace had also been calm, because Grey wasn't with Jace.

But that also didn't completely make sense. Jace had said that things hadn't changed, and that he was still dangerous. Most of the time when Fillip was chasing him, after he had told Grey that he didn't need him any more, he had been angry. But, Fillip was also almost positive that Grey had something to do with Jace's sudden changes of attitude. After all, the image in Martin's dream had hinted at the relationship.

When they had been in the fifth dimension for the first time, Jace had trapped Martin in his sleep. In his dream, Martin had a vision of a four-year-old child with a teddy bear, alone. Then Grey appeared, and had said, "Jace". Fillip couldn't believe that he hadn't figured it out before. Grey had transferred some of his anger and power into Jace, and possibly had been controlling him all along.

Stopping the Great
Shattering Device

_44_

Martin had only a slight memory of where
Mathanog and Soseph lived, but it wasn't good enough.
Jess created holographic radar that pinpointed where
Mathonog and Soseph lived, as she had stored that
information from the year before. Martin steered the
pod towards the home base of Mathonog and Soseph.

All that remained was to find out where
Mourndess was based, and then he could place a scan
in her house so he could keep track of her. Finding
Mourndess' station wasn't difficult. Once, Mathonog
had put Mourndess on a locator screen and Jess had
copied it in her memory. She could now create a
similar screen that indicated Mourndess' position. It
seemed that Mourndess was moving, which probably
meant that she was after the Shattering Device. Martin
followed.

Martin stayed far away from Mourndess.
He did not know if she had noticed him. If so, she

apparently didn't care. Eventually, Martin realized that Mourndess couldn't possibly have located the Shattering Device, but was instead still looking for it. Martin continued following her, waiting for something to happen. Within minutes, his sensors indicated some form a few thousand parmiles away. Ignoring the fact that Mourndess would surely see him, he maneuvered for a closer look and, for the third time in his life, he saw the Shattering Device. The two other instances were still etched clearly in his memory. The first had been from a satellite in the third dimension when he was a young man, and the second time had been when he had a vision of the device at a meeting the year before.

Martin saw that it was even more fantastic when he got to see it so closely and in real life. It was actually a very large, colorful spaceship. Its colors were continually changing. Occasionally it even changed to a color that he had never seen before, and then it would change again.

The Shattering Device could also shape shift, but this did not seem to alter its speed at any time. This confused Martin. He knew, as a scientist, that a large irregular ship should not be able to move in its atmosphere as well as a small sleek ship. Martin also noticed that when it changed shape, it never became completely flat, so there was always space inside. Martin was completely amazed at what he saw, and found himself remembering everything Mourndess had said about it.

That reminded him...Mourndess was still there! He snapped out of his trance. He realized that chances were good that Mourndess was going to try to use some kind of net to capture the device. Martin also had a net that would be able to catch another net and reel it back towards his pod. Because Mourndess' ship was probably stronger than Martin's, considering her more advanced technology so far, Martin would have to simply catch the net long enough to prevent Mourndess from capturing the device. Then he would release his net immediately so that Martin's ship did not get dragged into hers.

For a while Martin waited. Perhaps Mourndess was in awe of the Shattering Device like he was, although she had probably seen it many more times than he had. Perhaps she had realized that Martin was there and was trying to figure out a plan. Or, perhaps, she was simply trying to surprise him. Martin had not thought of that last possibility until Mourndess suddenly shot out her net towards the Shattering Device. Startled, Martin jammed the button that let his net out, and by pure luck, his net caught Mourndess' net perfectly, preventing her from capturing the device.

Martin sighed in relief and waited for Mourndess' net to start returning to her ship. Then he pressed the button to release her net from his grasp. Mourndess' ship started to rotate slightly towards Martin's pod. Martin was hoping that she was turning around and giving up, but that seemed unlikely. Mourndess' ship turned completely around until it faced Martin's. Then, her net came out and swung around until his pod was completely caught in Mourndess' net.

There were two bad things about that turn of events. First, Martin was now trapped, a prisoner, and therefore completely unable to prevent Mourndess from capturing the Shattering Device. Second, it was quite difficult to see. Martin and Jess were able to see only enough to know that Mourndess' ship had rotated around completely until she was facing the Shattering Device.

Martin could hear the noise of Mourndess' net coming out of her pod and heard the bump of the Shattering Device against his ship, indicating that the Shattering Device would be joining him for this ride. Martin didn't like this at all. Both he and Jess were speechless on their forced ride back to Mourndess' station.

The Truth

45

Fillip decided that, just as he had done the day before, he would go to see Jace with Dan, who had agreed to accompany him. But this time Fillip decided he would ask more specific questions. He thought about what those questions would be on the way there. It was close enough that Fillip and Dan felt no need to use a transporter. After the transporter accident that their mother had been lost in, no one in the family ever felt entirely safe with the transporters and used some other way of travel whenever possible, even though transporters had been modified since then and were safer.

Finally, they arrived at Jace's cell. Fillip was, again, permitted to enter, but this time the guard told Fillip to be cautious. The night before, the guard on duty in that room had reported that Jace had gone mad. The guard told Fillip that Jace had been screaming and bashing against the force field the entire night. The force field was actually wavering in a few spots

The damage was severe enough for them to reprogram the force field while the guards immobilized Jace to prevent him from escaping. The new force field was strong enough to withstand Jace's abuse. The guard then indicated that a human child could not possibly have damaged a force field like that. Fillip silenced him simply by saying,

"He's different than most people you keep here, okay?" When Fillip walked into Jace's cell he found him sitting on the ground, in the same position he had been in the last time Fillip had spoken with him. Fillip saw that this time Jace was crying.

"You damaged the force field," Fillip said to him. Jace didn't respond. Fillip continued, "Tell me, if you knew that once Grey had left you, you would start to change into the calm, scared..."

"I'm not scared of anything!" Jace screamed. "Not even death anymore. Whether I was doing the wrong thing or not, I was stronger, more powerful; it was better then. I thought that the part of me that Grey changed would stay forever, that I had been with him long enough for the effect to be permanent. Like the way I was last night, but forever. In a way, I was right, but I was also very wrong. I started changing, changing back into the person I was before Grey came to me.

"But, as long as Grey exists, I think that I may always revert back into who I was with Grey. I made a mistake, telling him I didn't need him any more. Now, I'm reverting back less and less, and to what good? Now, I can never be happy. Even when I was with Grey, I sometimes wondered what it would be like to be good, to change back into who I was before. But look at what good that did me! Look at me now! Just look!"

Fillip backed away just in time to avoid a punch that Fillip feared might have been able to kill him. He sat down and watched the transformation as Jace turned from a hopeless, scared, and confused nine-year-old boy turn back into a madman, bashing at the new, stronger force field. Fillip just sat there, watching, feeling there was not much else he could do except wait for Jace to return to the helpless boy again. Fillip wasn't leaving until he got his questions answered.

About an hour of screaming and banging later, Fillip watched as Jace turned back to the young boy, who just looked at Fillip and then fell to his knees in tears. Jace was learning for the first time how truly afraid he was of having a side of him that ruined his life, and that constantly wanted to take control over him. He was also learning that he could do nothing about it when he saw this happening. After a while, Jace sat up, wiping a last tear out of his eye and looking at Fillip.

"Can I ask you a few questions Jace?" Fillip asked him cautiously. Jace just looked at him as if he was speaking another language, and then slowly, started to nod his head. Fillip continued, "Do you know what Grey did to you to change you?"

"He lived in me, controlled me, for he found it much easier to get what he wanted when done through someone else; he...possessed me. And all the time, I was fully aware of what I was doing, as if I watched my life from when Grey first met me as a movie. But I did have some control, like when I told him I didn't... need...him. I slowly gained control and did things on my own; he could just tell me to do something without having to fully control my body, and often I did things without him telling me to. I could read his mind and knew what he wanted me to do.

"But it's different now. Now I don't even know what he wants me to do when I change into my, different side. I'm simply angry, powerful, and free to do whatever pleases me. Even though I know when I'm doing this that I shouldn't be doing it, and don't even want to be doing it, it is like rules and common sense don't matter to me any more. I'm not even really human when I change; I'm just like a younger, weaker, out of control Grey."

Jace finished and then there was silence. Jace was silent because he didn't want to go on with the subject any more and Fillip was silent because it was a lot of information to digest. Then, Jace spoke again, quiet and calm this time, "But, at least when I was with Grey, I mattered. I was only his tool, but I mattered. Look at me now, I don't matter at all, I'm useless and ruined. You should probably go home now, and be happy." But Fillip wasn't just going to leave like that. That wasn't the way that Fillip worked,

"I know someone who can make you matter again, someone who would be able to accept you even with your problem." Jace winced at that last word and then looked at Fillip and said,

"Leave me alone. You want to make me feel better, but it just isn't going to work. Just go home." Jace turned around and crossed his arms. One of the guards walked in and said,

"Is everything all right down here?" Fillip looked at him and said,

"Yes, we're fine." The guard shrugged and walked out of the room, closing the door behind him. Fillip looked back at Jace and said, "I'm telling the truth, really, I am."

But Jace wouldn't budge. "Believe me; you'll be much happier without getting involved with me, just go home!"

"NO!" Fillip shouted. Slowly, Jace turned around. Fillip continued, "I'm not leaving, because that's just not the person I am, okay? Now I'm not lying to you or trying to make fun of you, or anything. And if I mess up, then I'm going to suffer the consequences, not you! No, listen to me! I know someone who will take you in for free, and treat you like you were family, and make you matter again. That is you, as in who you're becoming, who you really are. He will live with whatever that decision might do, even though a little piece of Grey will always be with you, I promise."

Jace looked at him with a bit of hope in his eyes for the first time that Fillip had ever seen. Jace said, "Who would that be?"

Fillip stared at him directly in the eye and said simply, "Me."

Their Escape from her Trap

46

Once the door to his transport pod was opened, Martin was escorted to a prison by flying robots. They had laser blasters, and Martin realized that it would probably not be a good time to struggle. The robots had to be able to fly, because the ground outside the prison was covered with gluemax. Jess hid in his pocket as they took Martin to a cell, threw him in, and closed the door.

A few minutes later, Martin realized that the door could only be opened from the outside. But he had Jess. The cell was relatively complex. Apparently Mourndess enjoyed creating fool-safe cells. There were thick bars surrounded by a layer of weak plasma, creating a sharp sting when he touched the bar. The door was titanium and heavily plated, probably resistant to the elements.

The stone was hard and cold, with metal bars on the door. Not even Jess could bore through all that. Then, to make matters worse, the ground outside the cell was covered in gluemax. The gluemax didn't seem to be hardening, so it must have been replenishing itself from some secret source.

The room was long enough so that it would be impossible for anyone to make his way across the room without touching the ground. Martin noticed a tiny crack going through the middle of the floor but he wasn't entirely sure about it because the gluemax made it difficult to see the floor. There was a dial on the wall that he thought opened the door, but also might open up the crack so that there wasn't any ground anymore. Whoever turned that dial would then fall into a trap. But then, Martin had Jess.

When Martin was certain he understood the way in which the cell worked, he came up with a plan. He explained to Jess what he thought she had to do, and before she began, he said, "Go quickly. Mourndess has the Shattering Device and time is running out!" Jess nodded and began.

Mourndess was standing, looking at the Shattering Device. Finally, she had it. She alone had the device. She got up and started to walk around the device, looking at it carefully. It was a shame, she thought, that the device would be destroyed after it was used, for it would be great to keep it and be able to look at it day after day…She stopped walking and sighed. She supposed that she would have to get started, before Mathonog and Soseph found out that she had it. She looked up at the device's beauty once more, then opened the back portal and entered. She attempted to close the portal quickly behind her, but left it slightly open instead.

First, Jess flew through the bars with caution, just barely avoiding getting stung. Then, she flew to the end of the room where the dial was. She tried turning it, but it wouldn't budge. Martin said, "Try heating it to average body temperature. Perhaps it was made to be only opened by a human."

Jess heated it to body temperature and it worked. She turned the dial. As Martin had thought it would, the ground parted and the gluemax fell through. Jess waited a few seconds and the ground closed back up again. Then Jess went to go open the door. Like most other security latches, this one Jess was able to open by sticking her feelers into it and maneuvering the latch by flying in a circle. With a great deal of trouble, Jess flew Martin out of the room. They were determined to stop Mourndess, no matter what.

Mourndess and the Great Shattering Device

47

Martin had learned during his past vision that the Shattering Device contained many pulleys, gadgets, computers and an assortment of machines. That was exactly what Mourndess was seeing now. She had finished walking through the interior and was at the very front of the ship. She went to the main control panel and typed in the code that turned the device on. She began the ritual.

Martin found himself in another long hallway, but this one was much thinner and longer than the last, and fortunately this one wasn't covered in gluemax. Unfortunately, in this room there were twelve clawed security probes that didn't look very friendly. Martin had to decide what he was going to do before the probes attacked him. He grabbed the Connector and quickly created a fifth dimension warp. He tossed the Connector in a way so that it would land on top of the control panel, and then he grabbed Jess and jumped back out of the hallway, slamming the door behind him. He had no doubt that Jess could react fast enough to get out of the way. After all, she was a machine. Martin heard the sound of a warp appearing and disappearing, and then he re-entered the room. The twelve devices were gone and his Connector was sitting on the ground, a little scratched, but otherwise okay. He went over and picked it up. After he made sure Jess was all right, he pocketed the Connector and ran through the hallway to the next room.

Mourndess watched as lights appeared everywhere on the Device, and it slowly began operating. She then programmed the code that asked the Shattering Device to do what it was originally made to do. It then began to tell her that before it could complete the task, there was someone standing in its way, but she quickly skipped through that with another code. Then, there was just one more code to add, one that she now knew, which would once and for all help her complete her life-long quest. She put her fingers on the keypanel…

Martin ran out into a very large room that was entirely empty except for one thing: the Shattering Device. Martin ran as hard and fast as he could towards the device, noticing that there was the door in the back that was slightly open. Martin threw himself at the door at an angle that would both knock it open and get him inside the Device. This, he noticed, made Mourndess look up from the keypanel at him.

Then Martin felt the room getting very, very hot, and he knew it was even hotter for Mourndess. She was still trying to type, and was only a few symbols away from her goal. She screamed and fell down, panting and sweating from the heat. A device had fallen out of her pocket when she fell, and she just barely dragged herself towards the device. She activated a small heat reverser and a transparent blue layer surrounded her. She sighed in relief, the heat gone.

Jess stopped heating the ship and looked at Martin uncertainly. Jess supposed that it would be best to get Mourndess out of the Shattering Device so that she couldn't finish the code. So Jess flew over and grabbed Mourndess with her feelers, lifted her off the ground, and put her back down again outside of the Shattering Device. Martin walked out of the Shattering Device after Jess. The second he stepped out, the Shattering Device lifted off the ground and flew off into the distance.

Martin watched it and felt relief because he knew that, this time at least, Mourndess wasn't going to finish her quest. What Martin didn't know was that if the final code was entered incorrectly, the Shattering Device would make itself scarce and avoid capture for some time to come.

Martin and Jess ran to where their pod was waiting, jumped in and backed out of the space station that Mourndess called home. They flew away and then landed far from Mourndess' station. Martin and Jess got out of the pod and Martin made it small enough to fit in his pocket. He took out his Connector and set it for the third dimension.

Martin and Jess walked through the warp and found themselves at home. Neither Fillip nor Dan were home, which probably meant that they were still at the jail, with Jace. Martin pulled up a lounger near the door and sat down to wait for them to return. As he sat there, his dog at his feet, he started thinking over everything that had happened and remembering the Shattering Device and its beauty. Somehow he knew that this wouldn't be the last time he ever saw it.

A Second Chance

48

Fillip and Dan returned home from the jail a couple of hours later. Fillip didn't get to bring Jace with him because according to the jailer, Martin was the one who had complete control over Jace, not Fillip. Fillip had spent almost an hour arguing with him, but to no avail.

Fillip said to his dad, "Things happened while you were gone. What time did you get back?"

"Two hours ago."

"And because you are hours late, I'm assuming things happened to you as well. Let me tell you what happened first." And so he did. He described his conversations was Jace in vivid detail. Then Martin said,

"Wait a minute. You ran out to the fourth dimension and ran through the seventh, the eighth, the ninth, the tenth, the eleventh, the twelfth, and the thirteenth dimension to capture Jace. Then, a few days later you want to free him AND take him into our house?" Fillip nodded slowly and then said,

"Maybe we should discuss it after you tell us what happened to you."

"Okay," Martin said. Then he told them everything that had happened to him, with Jess adding in facts the Martin had not mentioned. Martin also spent quite a bit of time describing the Shattering Device to his children.

Once Martin had finished, Fillip and Dan said nothing. They wished very much that they had been there with Martin, to see the Shattering Device in person. Although Fillip and Dan were silent, Martin waited only a second before speaking again.

"Fillip, you're not serious, are you?" But Martin knew that Fillip was. It was just like Fillip, to do something like this. Fillip nodded his head and said,

"Yes, I'm very serious." Martin was silent after that. Then, Dan spoke,

"I really don't know what to say about this, but Fillip, could you tell us your reasons? Why do you want us to release Jace so badly, when a few days ago you wanted us to imprison him?" Fillip sighed, then said,

"When I wanted you to imprison him, I thought that he was truly mad, and barely even human considering the strength he displayed when I was chasing him. Now I know his secret, that he was possessed by Grey, that it wasn't his fault! Now he isn't possessed by Grey. Now he has nothing; he's returning to the kid he was supposed to be, to live a life behind bars for something he didn't have much control over. I was there, and saw that he wasn't crazy, or angry, or proud. You could tell that he was scared, confused, and miserable.

"Before I saw him as a criminal, as a madman. Now I see him as a kid, a nine-year-old kid who just lost the one figure in his life who he felt he mattered to. Now he really needs our help. Now that Grey isn't with him any more he almost has full control, I'm sure! Could we just give him a few days out of jail and if it doesn't work, we could put him back, or find him somewhere where he can live? Please?"

Martin and Dan looked at him, thinking over what he had said. Martin looked at Dan uncertainly.

"It sounds okay to me, I guess it is worth a try when he puts it that way," Dan said, responding to the look his father had given him.

Jess piped in, "It's all right with me, after what Fillip said. I still have some doubts, so we should try it for a few days before we make a final decision." Martin just looked from face to face, still not sure about it, but each of them were looking at him in such a pleading way…he cracked,

"All right, all right, but just for a few days. Then it's up to me entirely! Okay?" Fillip nodded with joy in his eyes. The dog had been sitting there, apparently listening to everything that was being said. He had a worried expression on his face.

The next day, Martin went to the jail with Fillip, Dan, and Jess. Martin told the jailer to release Jace, and told him that in a few days they would either return him or decide to keep him for a while longer. The jailer nodded, but with uncertainty. He went to Jace's cell and unlocked it. Martin, Dan, Fillip, and Jess had followed the jailer to the cell and were there when Jace was released. Then they walked back to the house with Jace, talking.

They decided that they would put Jace in school. The found out that Jace could read and write in many languages and knew quite a bit about science and engineering. He was good at inventing, as it was something that Grey did well too. He also knew a lot about the dimensions, but little about history. There was much that they could teach each other.

Soon after they got home, they went back to the fourth dimension to go to Jace's old home, where they packed some of his inventions and little else. Jace then returned to the third dimension with them. Later that day, something quite odd happened. They were just talking, and then Jace began transforming into his angry uncontrollable self, and started screaming. Immediately the dog walked into the room, as calm as ever. The dog stared at Jace and then Jace rapidly calmed down. They never said anything about how that had happened to Jace, but they all wondered about how their dog had done that. That dog clearly had impressive powers.

They decided that having Jace in their household wouldn't be that difficult if their dog could turn him back into a regular kid whenever he started to transform. Jace didn't ever talk about his relationship with their dog, but it seemed like they had known each other for a long time. And so Jace's new life began.

A Few Days Later...

So far, Jace had not been any bit of trouble at all. As a matter of fact, he had even told Martin about a few things he had made with Grey's help that Martin had brought to work. So, Martin agreed that Jace could stay with them, at least until he found some reason to make him leave. This decision made everyone much happier, especially Fillip and Jace. Everyday, Jace would just look at their dog, and then for the entire day he would remain calm and happy. Actually, unless something happened to make them change their minds, Jace's move was permanent.

Martin had been thinking almost constantly about what had been happening to him and his family. Right now, he was sitting in the living room with Fillip, Dan, Jess, Jace, and his dog, who was still unnamed. No one said anything. They simply enjoyed staying with each other for the company. Even though Martin knew that the Shattering Device would appear again, and that Mathonog and Soseph would bother him again, he felt certain that nothing was going to happen in the near future. He would set up fail-safe security systems to protect his friends and family. Somehow he knew that they would be safe for a while, and was happy for that.

Yet, he knew it wasn't over yet. He knew their journey had just begun.

About the Author

Jacob Salpeter Buckley is currently eleven years old, having just finished fifth grade. He wrote this book, which is a sequel to Traveling to the Fourth Dimension, over the course of one year. An avid reader and story teller, Jacob lives in Woodside, California with his parents, his brother Nick and his dog Big Chief Jolly. He has varied interests that include practicing and competing as a gymnast, traveling to interesting places, and writing very long sentences. He plans to be a writer when he grows up, and also wants to be an environmental attorney, a particle physicist, a math teacher, and a Jungian psychologist.